A Game of Spies

ALSO BY JOHN ALTMAN

A Gathering of Spies

A Game of Spies

John Altman

G. P. Putnam's Sons
New York

G. P. Putnam's Sons
Publishers Since 1838
a member of
Penguin Putnam Inc.
375 Hudson Street
New York, NY 10014

Library of Congress Cataloging-in-Publication Data

Altman, John, date.
A game of spies / John Altman.
p.   cm.
ISBN 0-399-14837-X
1. Intelligence officers—Fiction.   2. World War, 1939–1945—
Fiction.   3. Great Britain—Fiction.   4. Atomic bomb—Fiction.
5. Germany—Fiction.
PS3601.L85 G3   2002   2001-048192
813'.6—dc21

Printed in the United States of America
1   3   5   7   9   10   8   6   4   2

This book is printed on acid-free paper. ♾

BOOK DESIGN BY RENATO STANISIC

For Anicée

Thanks to Richard Curtis, my agent,
for his insight and guidance, and to Neil Nyren, my editor,
for his countless contributions to this book.

Overall, France and its allies turn out to have been better equipped for war than was Germany, with more trained men, more and better tanks, more bombers and fighters. . . . When Germany opened its offensive against the Low Countries and France in May 1940, not a single [German] general expected victory to result. The chief of staff of the German army wrote to his wife that his fellow generals thought what they were doing was "crazy and reckless." . . . But if the Allies in May 1940 were in most respects militarily superior, were not badly led, and did not suffer from demoralization (not yet, at least), then what accounts for Germany's six-week triumph?

—ERNEST R. MAY, *STRANGE VICTORY: HITLER'S CONQUEST OF FRANCE*

A Game of Spies

Prologue

MÜNCHEN-GLADBACH, GERMANY:
OCTOBER 1939

Hagen had not slept well; his head was throbbing with fatigue.

As the Mercedes limousine rolled toward the frontier, he reached into his breast pocket and withdrew a vial of SS *Sanitäts* aspirin. He thumbed it open, put two of the chalky pills into his mouth, and swallowed them dry. After returning the vial to his pocket, he turned to look at his companion, Major Schinkel. Schinkel appeared calm; his eyes were cool and haughty behind rimless spectacles.

Hagen, seeing this, allowed himself to relax. He leaned back in his seat, willing the aspirin to take hold. He was a pale, Scandinavian-featured man with close-cropped silver hair and a crook in his nose from a long-ago training session that had ended badly. Now, thanks to the restless night, his face looked unusually sunken: the skin drawn too tautly across the high cheekbones, the blue eyes looking out from deep hollows.

They passed through the German checkpoint with a friendly exchange—but the Dutch were less hospitable. The border guard scowled at the men's forgeries, held a hasty palaver, then ordered them out of the car. Now the aspirin were starting to take effect, and Hagen was able to watch the inspection with a genuine smirk on his face. There were no weapons in the Mercedes or on their persons. The weapons were in the next car, the one following ten minutes behind.

Presently, the Dutch could find no reason to keep the men delayed. They were waved back into the car and then waved on.

After another four minutes, the Mercedes drew to a stop before a two-storied gabled café, with potted plants on a balcony and a scatter of deserted garden chairs out front. Hagen and Schinkel exchanged a glance and then left the car without speaking. They navigated the chairs and moved inside, into a warm room filled with the clatter of silverware and the fragrance of fresh coffee.

The British had arrived ahead of them.

The men greeted one another with half-courtesies: the British half-standing, the Germans half-bowing. Hobbs, Hagen thought, looked as if he had not slept well himself. His sandy-blond hair was unkempt; his thin mustache looked more ruffled than usual. He seemed ill at ease in his chair, unable to fit his rangy legs comfortably beneath the table. But the other man, Dill, looked rested—fresh, and overly eager.

The Germans sat and ordered coffee. A spot of sunlight on the white tablecloth flickered slightly as a cloud drifted through the sky outside.

They picked up where they had left off, with Dill describing his network of brothers and cousins and sympathetic friends. Dill was not a working man, according to the story he had told the Germans. He had been on the dole for half his life, and had spent that time—cleverly, he seemed to think—cultivating a network against the British. His promises included wide-ranging campaigns of sabotage, espionage, and black propaganda. But Dill's brogue, Hagen noticed, had a tendency to wax and wane. He played his role with too much gusto, with too much hearty earthiness, betraying his true opinion of the Irish.

Hagen and Schinkel nodded encouragingly as Dill made his promises, then turned their attention to Hobbs. For the past decade, William Hobbs, according to his cover story, had squandered his time with a variety of pursuits—errand boy, factory worker, stonemason's apprentice, author of political pamphlets, and member of Owsley's British Union of Fascists. According to the cover story, he had also spent that time informing on his malfeasant peers for MI6. It was a fine act, Hagen thought, mixing fact and fiction in just the right proportions. The Germans had been watching British spies since the mid-1930s and already had Hobbs on file as a possible agent. It was entirely possible that a man cut from his cloth—part-time spy, part-time provocateur, full-time drinker and womanizer—would be swayed by a few reichsmarks to go over to the other side.

In reality, of course, it had taken much more than a few.

The spot of sunlight on the table was lost in a sudden flurry of similar spots. Hagen glanced up. Through the window, he could see the flared black fender of the second Mercedes as it pulled up outside the café.

He shot a look at Schinkel. The major was listening to Hobbs, looking appropriately disturbed at a demand the man had just made for more money. All for Dill's benefit, of course. According to the conditions of their agreement, Dill was to be returned to England unharmed within a week, at which point he would no doubt deliver a full report of this encounter to his superiors. So it had to look good.

"It may be possible," Schinkel was saying. "But we must have some collateral in exchange, I would think. Something to justify such an increase in expense."

Hobbs gave one of his lopsided, patronizing grins; he reached for a cigarette burning in an ashtray. "Herr Schinkel," he said cheerfully. "You insult me, sir."

Hagen's eyes drifted back to the window. The second Mercedes was waiting patiently. There were three men in the car, indistinct through the frosted windows.

At last Hobbs and Schinkel had hammered out an agreement—an extra fifty pounds, to be considered a bonus. Hagen stepped in quickly, bringing the meeting to a close before Dill could get any ideas about demanding more money for himself. It would be a waste of time, and time, with the second Mercedes waiting outside, was precious.

They settled their bill and gathered together their coats, then stood, offered more semi-bows, and shook hands all around. When they began moving toward the exit, Hagen and Schinkel hung back, letting the British go first. Hobbs walked with a slight limp—a trophy of a rugby injury, if Hagen remembered correctly, from many years before.

As soon as the men had stepped out into the sunshine, the doors of the second Mercedes swung open.

The three men who emerged from the car held the standard-issue Gestapo firearm, the Luger P 08.

They fanned out around the two Englishmen with the guns held at waist level. They wore plainclothes, dark and unexceptional. A few Dutch civilians milling in the street looked on, wide-eyed, as the Germans gestured the British toward the waiting car.

Hagen stayed near the patio of the café, cataloguing possible trouble spots, calculating chances of success. Hobbs would offer no problem, of course, because Hobbs was a willing part of the operation. But Dill would need to be watched closely. To Dill, the kidnapping would come as a rude surprise; and a man with his back to the wall, as Hagen well knew, was a man capable of anything.

His eyes moved to the Dutch civilians. They were gaping, plainly staggered by the Germans' effrontery. Holland was a neutral territory, and the spectacle before them now was so unexpected, so barefacedly illegal, that it had paralyzed them. They were sheep, Hagen thought, with a quick flash of disdain. There was nothing to fear there.

One thick-shouldered Dutchman, however, had a look in his eyes—a glimmer of courage. He would bear watching.

Now Hobbs was being forced into the car at gunpoint. Dill, waiting for his turn, was cursing bitterly at the three Gestapo agents. His hands were raised, perched on either side of his narrow, apple-cheeked face. He was looking for a chance, Hagen thought. But would he be stupid enough to take one?

Evidently he was. In the next instant, Dill had shoved one of the Gestapo full on the chest. As the man tumbled backward, he made a sudden, frantic break to his right.

Hagen swore to himself, and moved to intercept.

Too slow. The two Gestapo still standing raised their guns and fired in unison. The reports sounded flat, rolling off down the quiet street and then echoing back. Dill crumpled forward with a bright red flower spreading between his shoulder blades.

The door of the Mercedes slammed shut, sealing off Hobbs.

Hagen moved to check on the wounded Britisher. Still alive. He waved at the Gestapo to come and give him assistance, then bent down and began to wrestle Dill to his feet.

From the corner of his eye, he saw the beefy Dutchman coming forward—he had found the courage somewhere.

Hagen straightened. He left Dill to the SS and moved to deal with the Dutchman himself. He circled around behind the man, raising his hand and forming a knife edge, tucking the thumb into the palm, preparing to deliver a single blow to the base of the neck.

Before he could complete the act, another gun had fired. The Dutchman's head whipped back; the air behind him clouded with crimson mist.

Hagen swore again.

Complications.

He hated complications.

When he looked back over his shoulder, Dill, limp as a rag doll, was being manhandled into the waiting car. The doors closed and the Mercedes pulled away with screaming tires.

Hagen took one last look at his surroundings—the Dutchman with his ruined head pulsing out gouts of blood, the bright rust-colored spot left in the street by Dill, Major Schinkel standing with a dazed look on his face. Then he raised a hand to his temple. His headache was back, sharper than before.

He and Schinkel hurried to their own car. Now engines were revving in the distance. A siren rose, hovered, and languidly fell. Hagen slapped the back of the driver's seat. "Go!"

They went.

The Mercedes with the prisoners would simply barrel through the checkpoint without stopping. Hagen decided they would do well to follow suit. He wondered if Dill was mortally wounded. He wondered if the Dutch would follow them over the border. He decided to instruct the German border guard to open fire if they tried it. This had never happened, after all. The Dutch had no reason for violating German territory.

He looked again at Major Schinkel. Schinkel still looked dazed. Hagen gave him a reassuring smile. He reached into his pocket and withdrew the aspirin and dry-swallowed two more.

Complications or not, things had gone well enough. The British were in their custody, and Dill—if he survived—would have no reason to suspect Hobbs of complicity.

"Success," he said.

Schinkel gave his head a small shake. He looked on the verge of vomiting.

Hagen kept smiling. Now that it was over, he felt extremely calm. Even the headache was receding again.

There was nothing he liked better than a successful operation.

Part One

Chapter One

THE HAVEL RIVER, BERLIN:
FEBRUARY 1940

Each time a Berliner moved in her direction, Eva Bernhardt's heart picked up speed in her chest.

An old man with a cane and monocle . . . a young man riding a bicycle with a great mane of unruly dark hair billowing out behind . . . a middle-aged couple pushing a baby carriage; any of them might have been her contact. But she did not want to attract attention, so she kept her face neutral and her hands folded in her lap. On the bench beside her was a newspaper, *Der Stürmer*, which she had already read from front to back. It was filled with vitriolic attacks on the Jew devil, the mongrel Russian, and the pygmy Czech. In other words, the usual.

Today, as for the past several months, the park's inhabitants—like most of the inhabitants of Berlin—were eerily calm. They were poised on the edge of a knife blade, Eva thought, waiting to see on which side they would fall. If Hitler dragged them into a war, they would be dragged, for it was too late to turn back. But they were not anxious for war. In a month or two, perhaps, if things went well in the West, they would not remember having not been anxious for war. If things went well in the West, they would be only too happy to forget their hesitations and claim their prize. But if things went poorly, they would remember it differently: as something nobody had wanted, as something they had all been helpless to avoid.

A man was wandering toward the bench.

She stole a glimpse of him. He was somewhere around forty, balding, wearing a black trench coat, walking with a silver-headed cane. She made herself look away as he drew closer.

Then he was moving past, muttering something to himself, trailing a snatch of singsong cadence.

She forced air out between clenched teeth and kept waiting. The wind gave a sudden gust, teasing a strand of auburn hair from beneath her tight-fitting snood. She tucked it back in mechanically. Her hands wanted to keep moving: to rub nervously at the skin beneath her turquoise eyes, or fidget with the tails of her plain cloth coat. She forced them to hold still.

The man with the silver-headed cane paused. He turned, shuffled back toward the bench, and smiled at her.

"Good afternoon," he said.

"Good afternoon," Eva said.

"I wonder if you could direct me to something, young lady. The *KaDeWe* department store."

Her heart flip-flopped in her chest.

"You'll need to take a taxi," she answered easily. "Have you shopped there before?"

"Not for many years."

"Make a point to visit the seventh floor."

"Walk with me," he said under his breath.

She stood, her heart still pounding urgently, and picked up her newspaper.

For a few moments they strolled without speaking. She sneaked glances at the man beside her as they walked, trying to figure him out. He was a German—a lifelong Berliner, judging from his accent, although of course that was only speculation. What had made this man go to the other side? He had not lived in England, she guessed, as she had. Perhaps he had been seduced by somebody. MI6 had many tactics at their disposal, but seduction, the oldest and simplest, was often the most effective. It had been the tactic, after all, that had worked so successfully on Eva herself.

She soon abandoned this theory. The man did not strike her as that type. He struck her as a family man—she noticed a wedding band on one pale hand—who perhaps had children. He was doing this for the noblest reasons, she decided. He wanted his children to grow up in a world where neighbors did not turn on neighbors. Or perhaps he was a Jew, or a half-Jew, or he was married to a Jew. The possible reasons were legion. Most surprising was that there were not more like this man, more like herself.

After walking for a few dozen yards, the man used his cane to indicate another bench. "Let's sit."

They sat. Eva sent a nervous glance around, looking for Gestapo. She saw none—but that was hardly reassuring. The core of the Gestapo's organization was not stormtroopers, after all, but ordinary citizens: informers, hausfraus, and gossips eager to cultivate favor.

The man was unwrapping a cigar he had taken from his pocket. He put it into his mouth, lit it from a dog-eared matchbook, and puffed on it twice.

"There is a man," he said mildly, "named Klinger. A clerk for OKW, and a veteran of the Great War. Our benefactors believe he has some high-ranking friends at Zossen—fellow veterans who have applied themselves to their careers with more concentration than Klinger himself."

Eva nodded, almost imperceptibly.

"These friends," the man continued, "may possibly have access to details concerning the Wehrmacht's drive to the West."

She nodded again. At some point over the past few months, the Wehrmacht's drive to the West had become a foregone conclusion. Not so long before, things had been different. Not so long before, it had been easy to believe that Hitler's only real goal had been the absorption of the Germanic territories: Austria, the Sudetenland, and Czechoslovakia. This goal had struck most Germans as logical, even reasonable. Who could have blamed the Nazis for trying to reunify the ancient Germanic tribes, after the treaty of Versailles had heaped such injury and insult upon them? Who could have blamed them for trying to regain what rightfully had always been theirs?

Beneath this line of reasoning had run an unspoken current. If a larger war was to come, then it would come with the Russians, the *Untermenschen*, and not with the civilized people to the West. Expansion to the East was where Germany's true destiny lay. Hitler had always made this clear, even when he had been nothing but a failed street artist and a proselytizing convict. He had laid out his plans in plain black and white in the pages of *Mein Kampf*.

But then those in the West had made it clear that they would stand up to German aggression in Poland, after having not stood up so spectacularly at Munich, and as a result they had drawn Hitler's attention in their own direction. The Führer had conducted some hasty diplomacy, and suddenly everything had changed. The Nazi-Soviet pact had been signed, effectively closing off the East as an option, at least for the time being. Poland had been divided as spoils of war between the new, uneasy allies. And now Hitler's Wehrmacht was focused toward Belgium, Holland, and France—and beyond that, England. The Low Countries would fall easily. Once France had gone, the British would have no choice but to make peace. So now it was only a matter of time.

"Klinger," the balding man went on after a few moments, "is not the most ambitious of men. He likes his vices too much. Until now he's been a loyal, if uninspired, soldier of the Reich. But our benefactors have discovered an interesting fact about Herr Klinger—one that makes them look at him in a slightly different light." The man paused. "It concerns his father."

Two riders on horseback, wearing military regalia, were approaching the bench. The man fell silent until they had passed. Eva's eyes followed the horses longingly. Once she had ridden a great deal herself—long ago, when she had been very young, when the world had seemed filled with simple pleasures.

"The elder Klinger was a professor at the University of Berlin," the man said quietly. "A teacher of the natural sciences. When the Reich Minister of Education began to force the curriculum of *Rassenkunde* on the faculty, however, Herr Klinger resisted."

His eyes were unfocused, staring into the middle distance. He took the cigar from his lips and exhaled a stream of blue-tinged smoke into the wind.

"He was outspoken with his criticism. One night in 1934, he vanished. He has not been heard from since."

My people, Eva thought darkly.

"Now. Our benefactors have no particular reason to believe that Herr Klinger is anything but faithful to the Reich. The fate of his father, however, leads them to speculate that perhaps he harbors certain . . . feelings . . . which he has kept to himself."

Eva murmured assent.

"If the man *did* have such feelings—and if he *was* acquainted with certain higher-ranking men at Zossen, who would be capable of gleaning hints about Hitler's plans . . ."

"I understand," she said.

"Good. But you must tread softly. We do not know just where his loyalties lie."

"Yes."

"As I said: Klinger likes his vices. He can often be found at the bar of the Hotel Adlon after working hours, drinking and looking for women. He also likes his wife. But she exacts a high price for his infidelities. Jewels and furs. Herr Klinger is in rather serious debt. There are, you can see, several possible avenues of approach here."

Eva nodded once more, and began to twist a lock of hair around her index finger.

"You must present him with an opportunity—a chance to remove himself from his financial straits, and at the same time to seek justice for the fate of his father."

"Yes."

"But softly—softly."

"Yes."

"Time is of the essence," the man said. "Our benefactors are watching the weather. When it warms sufficiently, time will be up. We will meet again in one week at this bench. You'll apprise me of your progress then."

They sat for another minute in silence. Then the man stood, creakily. He put the cigar back between his lips. "Klinger is forty-five," he said. "Short. Dark. With a mustache just turning gray. The seventh floor?"

"I highly recommend it."

"Thank you, young lady. There are five hundred marks in the newspaper, to help you along. If Klinger proves valuable, more can be arranged. *Auf Wiedersehen.*"

"*Auf Wiedersehen*," she said.

She watched as he moved away, haltingly, leaning on the cane. She kept watching until he was out of sight. Then she stood, folding the newspaper under her arm, and strolled slowly away in the other direction.

After a moment, a man sitting on a nearby bench came to his feet. He folded his own newspaper beneath his arm, pulled the brim of his hat lower over his face, gave Eva another moment to gain some distance, and then fell into step behind her.

LAKE WANNSEE, DÜSSELDORF

Hagen could feel another headache coming on.

He reached for the bottle of SS *Sanitäts* aspirin and twisted off the lid. He was going through the little aspirin bottles quickly these days—too quickly. It would have concerned him, if only he'd had the time to be concerned by such trivialities.

He took two of the pills, added a third, and washed them down with the last cold sip of ersatz coffee in the mug by his hand. He returned the vial to the drawer of his desk and sat still, waiting for the headache to soften a bit before he proceeded to the next bit of unpleasantness on his roster for this altogether unpleasant day.

Around him, the villa was filled with the soft, professional sounds of business progressing as usual. In a room to his left, spies were being trained: he could hear the muted whir of cameras and the intermittent crackling of radio sets. Farther down the hall, a sample interrogation was proceeding in polite, gilded tones.

The villa, a sprawling holiday resort of several dozen rooms, had been built in 1914 but only recently had been taken over by the SS Security Service—Hagen's organization, the SD, or Sicherheitsdienst. Until a few months before, he thought, the sounds in the villa must have been very different indeed, as wealthy Berliners on vacation had slept, dined, played cards, and made love.

But times changed.

These days more than ever, times changed.

After a few minutes, the headache lost its edge, settling in for the duration as a dull thud. Hagen decided he could wait no longer. But the energy required for the task before him, which once would have been available in surfeit, felt beyond his grasp. Over the past few months, for the first time in his life, he had started to feel his age. The problem, no doubt, was a lack of activity. He sat behind this desk day after day, wrangling over minutia and nonsense.

He recognized, however, that he was no longer a young man. And he intended to age gracefully, if that was possible for a soldier such as himself. The time for active involvement in operations had passed. The maneuver in Holland had been his last. His legacy would come in the form of a pupil, a piece of clay to be molded in his image. And he had accepted this fact, as dispiriting as it sometimes seemed.

After a few moments, he exhaled a long, measured breath. He had been working too hard, he thought. He was feeling philosophical, and at his core he was not a philosophical man. A vacation was in order. If he could force himself to relax, things would look brighter.

A vacation. Still more idleness.

His lips pursed. After another moment, he summoned his resolve, shoved his chair back from the desk, straightened his dark tailored suit, and left the office.

He found William Hobbs standing on a balcony outside his room, facing the gray waters of Lake Wannsee and smoking a cigarette.

Hobbs was a large man, well over six feet tall, and fit, with an ex-athlete's build that was just starting to tend toward fat. He had a defeated look about him today, Hagen thought: tired and jaded and weary-eyed, with his sandy-blond hair teased into a rat's nest by the wind.

Hagen joined him by the railing, lighting a cigarette of his own. For several moments, neither man spoke. The water of the lake lapped quietly in the breeze. Finally, Hobbs cleared his throat.

"You've got something to tell me," he said.

He spoke roughly—proud of his humble roots, Hagen thought; eager to identify himself as East End instead of Oxford.

Hagen considered suggesting that they move inside, out of the wind, to have their conversation. But Hobbs looked settled in, somehow at home against the gray lifeless background. It would be easier to give the man the news here.

"I've received word from Reichsleiter Himmler," Hagen said. "You're not to be allowed to leave Germany—at least, not for the immediate future."

Hobbs said nothing. His broad shoulders sagged a bit as his eyes continued to scan the lake. The news could not have come as a surprise, of course. By now he must have been expecting it. But it was one thing to expect such news and another to hear it said aloud. Hagen gave the man a minute before continuing.

"In time we may make a different arrangement. But for now you're to remain with us. We'll be finished with the debriefing in another few days; then you'll go to Berlin." He paused. "I'll see to it that you're taken care of there."

Again Hobbs said nothing.

"You have my apologies," Hagen said. "But you must understand, it is out of my hands."

Hobbs took a final, vicious drag from his cigarette and then flicked it off the balcony. "Were you given a reason?" he asked.

"It seems you are considered a security risk."

"Even after my contributions here?"

Hagen shrugged.

Now Hobbs turned to face him more fully. A crooked smile played across the man's mouth. There was something self-hating in that smile, something so bitter that it was difficult to look at straight on.

"But surely, Herr Hagen, there's something I could do to change the situation. Give me a moment. I'll think of it."

Hagen knew what the man was driving at. The implication was that they were pulling out on the deal only to increase the strength of their bargaining position. The extension of that implication suggested a desire to insert Hobbs back into England as a double agent, to continue spying for the SD.

Hagen very nearly gave the man an answer: that Himmler and Heydrich did not trust Hobbs that far. Returning him to England as a double agent had been too tempting an opportunity to reject out of hand—they had genuinely hoped that he would impress them with his trustworthiness. But now, after four months of debriefing, Hobbs had done little to impress them. He drank too much and the information he provided was faulty, often contradictory. He was a man with few scruples and no real loyalties. He was also a dangerous man, trained at tradecraft by MI6, the most practiced espionage organization in the world. And so the decision to ship him off to Berlin, where he would be out of harm's way and available for the future, was not a bargaining tactic. It was non-negotiable.

Before he could say this, however, Hobbs rushed on:

"If you've got in mind what I think you've got in mind, then my price just went up."

A faint smile tugged at Hagen's lips. Hobbs the play-actor had said much the same thing, he was remembering, back at the café in Holland.

"We've got nothing in mind," he said, "except exactly what I've said."

"That's ridiculous. Think of what I could offer."

"The decision is out of my hands."

Hobbs stared at him for a moment, hard. Then he lit another cigarette and turned to look again at the lake.

"Tell me," he said slowly. "Am I really to be sent to Berlin? Or am I to be sent somewhere else—more permanent?"

"You will be settled in Berlin. A nice little apartment on Leipziger Strasse. And presently you will receive your money and your resort. All that has changed is the timing."

Hobbs looked unconvinced.

"It is not as bad as you seem to think. You will live well in Berlin. You will have money. A woman, if you like."

Hobbs snorted.

"We appreciate the value of your contribution," Hagen said. "It will not be forgotten."

"Dill died for this, you know."

Hagen said nothing.

"Dill had a son. I was his godfather."

Hagen held his tongue.

"Bloody hell," Hobbs said colorlessly, and tossed his cigarette, barely smoked, off the balcony.

"Come inside," Hagen suggested. "We have some final matters to discuss before the move can be implemented."

For a moment, Hobbs didn't react. Then he grunted. His broad shoulders slouched even lower, and he turned to follow Hagen back into the villa.

Chapter Two

THE HOTEL ADLON: MARCH 1940

Tonight would be the night.

Eva made the decision upon finishing her second *Rauchbier*. The beer was watered down but still went straight to her head: she felt tipsy, fluttery, and somewhat naughty. She allowed the naughty feeling to show on her face. Klinger, of course, would also need to know that tonight would be the night. How did the old saying go? It took two to tango.

Otto Klinger, sitting beside her at the bar of the Hotel Adlon, had one hand resting on her knee. He was kneading the flesh there absently as he spoke about his Iron Cross.

"Later on, they replaced the silver with silver trim. Some of the very last medals were cast from one piece, and had no silver at all. They were brass. Brass! But mine, Eva darling, is a real one. Pure silver. A beautiful piece of craftsmanship. Sometime I really must arrange to show it to you. . . ."

Klinger was shaped like a barrel, short and thick, with a salt-and-pepper mustache and an easy smile. *A charmer*, Eva thought. He reminded her of Hobbs in that way. His mustache was almost as fastidiously well kept as Hobbs' had been; he carried himself with a similar swagger. And his disarming smile, like Hobbs', had no doubt toppled many a young woman into many a bed over the years.

But she did not think about Hobbs anymore, if she could help it.

She forced herself to focus on Klinger.

She had met him at this same bar almost three weeks before, stationing herself beside the man rather shamelessly. He had chatted her up at once—after slipping his wedding ring unobtrusively into a pocket of his cheap suit—and with a great deal of suavity. Eva had found herself enjoying the experience, giving subtle indications of interest and then backtracking almost immediately. She had made him work for it.

Klinger had promptly mentioned his position at OKW, managing to make it sound like much more than clerk's work, and had then mentioned his service during the Great War, alluding to the Iron Cross he had been awarded. This, she realized later, had been the groundwork for his proposition. After an hour of conversation, on that first night, he had suggested that she might like to see his Iron Cross sometime. If she was interested, perhaps they could arrange a rendezvous. At this moment, he was late for a meeting—his meeting, no doubt, was supper with his wife—but he would very much like to share his Iron Cross with her at some point in the near future.

Eva had given him a heavy-lidded stare. She had surprised herself with her ability to play the cool seductress. After all, she had always been a quiet girl. But this other identity had been lurking just beneath the surface, it seemed, waiting patiently for a chance to come out. No doubt this was what Hobbs had seen in her: a hint of promise, a gleam of natural talent. An instinct for the game, that she had not even seen within herself.

And it was *fun.* She felt like Marlene Dietrich. Perhaps she had less to work with: her cheeks were not quite hollowed to perfection, and her eyes, no matter how she tried, refused to smolder. But at least half of the act, she was coming to realize, had nothing to do with physical beauty. It had more to do with attitude. And the attitude, she had. She had been perfecting it for years as recreation—practicing emotions in front of the mirror, miming feelings she had read off of others' faces. Long-suffering patience, from her mother—a small down-turning of the lips, with a glint of drowsy joy in the eyes to balance the frown. From her father, the opposite: spirited impatience, because the fields never did exactly what he wanted them to do. Over the dinner table or at night in front of the fire, he had projected a constant desire to get back to work, to forgo such human weaknesses as sleep and food, and instead concentrate entirely on his farm.

The small tricks of expression had been gathering, without her realizing it, into quite a nice little arsenal. From the girls at the dance halls—prettier girls than she—the careless toss of the hair and the demure aversion of the eyes. From her fellow governesses in England, the impeccable posture, the pretense of propriety that made one wonder what lay beneath. And from Hobbs himself, the illusion of confidence, of not caring much one way or the other. There was nothing more certain to attract attention than the illusion of not caring.

At some point, she had allowed, she might like to see Klinger's Iron Cross. But she did not think a rendezvous for the purpose was quite in order.

After that, it had been an easy matter to reel him in.

They had met twice more at the bar of the Adlon, seemingly by chance, and although Klinger had neglected to bring his medal, he had pressed her fervently for the outside tryst. Now she had decided that tonight would be the night. Until now, Hobbs had been the only lover of her life. The prospect of taking another, despite the obvious complications, was darkly thrilling.

"Not that I've got anything against the Party," Klinger was saying. "The Nazis have done some fine things for this city. Fine things. Once upon a time, this very bar would have been overrun by homosexuals, you know—sixteen-year-old boys in lederhosen with their cocks hanging out. And the streets outside would have been overrun by whores. Not the few you see these days—the ones that come out like rats to take advantage of the blackout— but whores by the dozen. Goebbels has done a fine job of cleaning up the city. But does that mean I need to join the Party? I think not. They're doing just fine without me."

Could he sense that Eva had made her decision about tonight? She thought he could. His hand, working at her knee, felt knowing.

"But they've done wonders in cleaning up the city," Klinger said. "Sex is best left indoors—out of public view." He grinned at her. "Eh?"

She smiled back at him.

"Eh?" he said again, and his hand moved slowly up her thigh.

"Absolutely," she said, and raised her glass to cover the smile before it could crack.

When it was over, Klinger pushed himself off the bed and wandered into the kitchen. Eva lay still, listening, as he fixed drinks.

She had done it. It was finished.

And it had not been so bad.

In fact, it had been rather nice. Klinger was very different from Hobbs. He smelled different, he moved differently, and he held her differently. And there was less at stake—in her heart, if not in the larger scheme of things—which left her free to enjoy the experience more. With Hobbs, after all, she had been in love. She had believed that she would have only one lover in her life, the man she would marry. As a result she had put terrific pressure on herself to enjoy the time spent in bed with him. When she had failed, she knew that she had disappointed them both.

But with Klinger the sex was nothing but a pleasant diversion. It hardly mattered whether the girl lying beneath him was Eva or somebody else. And that phenomenon, although she never would have expected it, had made things . . . well, nice.

Not terrific.

But nice.

Besides—Hobbs had never truly loved her at all. In retrospect their love affair had been revealed for what it was: a cynical and manipulative thing on his part, and a naive one on hers. If Hobbs had truly loved her, after all, would he have sent her away, back to Germany? Would he have endangered her, separated himself from her? Of course not.

He had never loved her. He had only recruited her.

Klinger came back into the room and handed Eva a glass. She propped herself up on one elbow and took a tentative sip. He had mixed a Razzle-Dazzle, a drink that was becoming increasingly popular in Berlin these days, thanks to the lack of supplies. It consisted of wood alcohol and grenadine. She pulled a face, then took another sip anyway.

Klinger collapsed onto the bed beside her, naked, somehow managing to avoid spilling his own drink. His hands began to roam again. For a man his age, she thought, he possessed admirable ardor.

"Eva," he said. "You are something, *Liebling.* You are something special."

She took another sip of her Razzle-Dazzle, and said nothing.

"You make a man feel young again," Klinger said. With that, he struck off on more reminiscences of his youth, of his days during the Great War. He seemed nostalgic for it—but, strangely, less than eager about the Great War that lingered even now on the horizon. Perhaps this was simply because he was too old to be a footsoldier. Or perhaps it was something else, something that Eva had sensed among many of her countrymen. They had been behind the First War completely, body and soul. They had taken to the streets to proclaim their enthusiasm in parades and celebrations. This new war was Hitler's battle, not theirs . . . not, at least, until it started going well.

But it was possible, she thought, that Klinger's lack of enthusiasm for the war ran deeper than that. To know for certain, she would need to get a better sense of the man, of where his true values lay.

Time is of the essence, her contact had said.

But also: *You must tread softly.*

She listened, enjoying the sound of his voice and the feel of his hand on her skin. She had been alone for so long that any human company was welcome. Ever since her return to Germany, she had kept a studious distance from coworkers and neighbors and prospective friends, afraid to let anyone get too close. She had not even told her own parents that she had come back. But the isolation had taken a toll. Her need for companionship had become something disconcertingly close to desperation.

Klinger, at least, was not such bad company. He liked to talk.

"Berlin is terribly *normal* for a city at war—don't you think? The cafés and the beer halls are all still open. The theaters are still playing American cinema. Last week I saw a Mickey Mouse movie. Mickey Mouse!" He laughed. "Not quite what one expects when one's at war—hm?"

The question seemed to be rhetorical; he talked on without waiting for an answer. Despite the man's garrulous nature, unfortunately, he had kept most of his secrets to himself. He had not yet told her that he was married. He had mentioned his job at OKW only to pique her interest at the beginning, and since then had not returned to the subject. Most important, he had not told her of his debts. This would provide an opening, if and when he decided to reveal it. But first they would need to grow closer, much closer than they were now. Why would he tell a young lady he was trying to impress that he was poor?

You must tread softly.

She listened, nodding at the right times, still enjoying his hand on her belly. He mentioned jokingly, in passing, that his only goal in life was to earn a tremendous amount of money, enough to buy himself a title. Von Klinger. She giggled and let it pass. It was still too soon. Next time . . .

"But you never talk about *your* life, Eva, *your* work. Where did you say it was?"

She blinked, then told him about the propaganda ministry, and about how tiresome and dull her time there was. It seemed that her years spent in England had qualified her only to pore over endless newspaper advertisements, searching for faint clues to the state of British morale. It was nothing to compare to the excitement of his position with OKW. . . .

He hardly seemed to have been listening. His hand was moving lower now, below her belly. He set his drink aside and dropped his cigarette into it, creating a sibilant hiss.

"Why must we talk of these things?" he murmured. "Why must we waste our time together talking of work?"

He was kissing her breasts, then moving down and kissing her belly. She set her own drink aside. Lay her head back on the pillow, closing her eyes.

She had introduced the concept, at least, of being dissatisfied with her work at the Rundfunk. Now she would let his own mind worry at the subject for a while. Deep down, he must want more than just a title; he must. Deep down, he must want justice.

She made herself lie still and accept the man's favors.

You must tread softly.

LEIPZIGER STRASSE

William Hobbs stood by the window, watching.

In the course of ten minutes, he saw a few pedestrians, scurrying like mice; a few black-suited SS men strolling as if they owned the sidewalk—which in a way they did—and two prostitutes. The prossies were out early tonight, Hobbs thought. But then, the prossies had been coming out early more and more often lately. Enforced blackouts were like gold to whores and thieves.

He kept watching as twilight settled across the city. The twilight was preternaturally clear, partially as a result of the blackout, with a plump alabaster moon materializing overhead. Under Hobbs' gaze, the evening crowd melted into the streets, jacketed and coifed, as if nothing out of the ordinary was going on. The sounds of conversation and occasionally even laughter drifted on the night air. They were determined to have fun, he thought, for as long as it was humanly possible. And for that he couldn't blame them—he felt in dire need of a drink or two himself.

He had not left this flat for twenty-three days now.

For the past twenty-four hours, he had been sharing it with a corpse.

After looking out the window for another moment, he turned and crossed the apartment, moving with a slight limp. He opened the icebox and crouched in front of it. His stomach executed a slow, queasy roll. He closed the icebox again and crossed back to the window. He couldn't eat—not with Borg in the room.

Borg lay near the bookcase, on his back, with one hand flung over his head like a man sunbathing on a beach. The pool of blood beneath him had coagulated during the course of the day, turning a rich, organic brown.

Hobbs returned to looking out the window. His hazel eyes, a shade lighter than his hair, moved back and forth in steady arcs. There was nobody watching the apartment from the street. He knew this for a fact because he had spent the past week making sure of it. For the first two weeks of his imprisonment—for imprisonment was what it was, regardless of what the Nazis chose to call it—a Gestapo agent had kept an eye on the apartment from the far street corner. As of nine days ago, however, the man had vanished. Hagen had evidently decided that Hobbs was secure enough under Borg's vigilant eye.

Hobbs kept looking for watchers anyway. As soon as full dark had fallen, he would make his bid for freedom, and he had no desire to end up in the basement of Prinz Albrecht Strasse, in the hands of the Gestapo interrogators.

He raised one finger to his mouth and began to nibble on the ragged cuticle.

He should have gone last night—immediately after killing Borg.

But he had lost his nerve. He had dawdled for too long, under the pretense of thinking it through from every angle, and by the time he had found his courage, the sun had been rising. So he had been forced to wait through another day, although he had been extremely conscious, painfully conscious, of the time slipping away.

Three months had passed since he had sent the letter to the cover address in Lisbon—to a sister, according to the story he had told Hagen, back in the days when they had still been playing nice with each other. The letter had contained no codes, and no secret messages; the simple fact of its dispatch had been the trigger for the next phase of the operation. Once the letter had arrived, Eva would be activated. And so by now Hobbs should have liberated himself, so that he would be able to shoulder his part of the burden: watching her back and, using the radio transmitter in the possession of his contact family, arranging the extraction.

But it had taken him nine days, after the Gestapo had stopped watching the flat, to summon the courage to kill Borg. It was not an easy thing, killing a man. Oldfield had warned him of that—and yet despite the warning, Hobbs had underestimated the difficulty involved.

Perhaps he was already too late. Perhaps Eva had already fallen into their clutches. Perhaps this was all for nothing.

Full dark descended in dribs and drabs; lights blazed to life behind blackout shades. Hobbs' eyes continued following the pedestrians as they came onto the streets. A couple walking arm in arm. An older gentleman with a bristly, fashionable Hitler mustache. A group of young women, doing their best to look glamorous without makeup or expensive clothes. They made him think of Eva; and that led his mind to the German named Teichmann.

If not for Teichmann, Hobbs would not have found himself in this room in Berlin with a dead man.

Teichmann, a double agent who had been working for both the British and the Germans, had been the one who had revealed that the entire official network of MI6 agents in Germany had been compromised—by Teichmann himself. By now, the man would have hanged for it. Hobbs hoped it had not been a clean hanging. Sometimes, he knew, the neck did not break immediately. Sometimes it took hours to die: a slow, painful strangulation.

He hoped the man had suffered.

Eva, however, had not been given up by Teichmann; for she had been part of a separate network, a set of sleeper agents who numbered only six. Oldfield's own show, kept separate from the rest of MI6 operations. British Intelligence was not above a few power games of their own. Nothing to compare with the endless machinations of Hitler's intelligence services, from what Hobbs had gathered during his time at the SD villa; Oldfield and his peers only had to worry about their careers and their reputations, not their lives. But careers and reputations *were* lives, in the hoary old halls of Whitehall, and so games were played, secrets kept. And it was a good thing, he supposed. Had things been different—had the old boffins around Leconfield House played all their cards above the board—then Eva would not be free at this moment. She would have been just another domino in the official MI6 network, a network that had come tumbling gloriously down.

But Eva had not been in contact with the British, during her time in Germany. She had been kept apart, waiting for her activation signal to come over the BBC, at which point she would rendezvous with her contact at a prearranged place, at a prearranged time.

The operation had come together over three long days spent at Whitehall.

Hobbs and Oldfield had devised the plan together. They would activate Eva and send her after the OKW clerk, Klinger. The need for intelligence concerning the invasion had, by then, become undeniable. Teichmann's revelation had closed off all the usual avenues. But Eva, and the few like her, were the aces up Oldfield's sleeve.

Yet by sending Eva to meet with her contact they would risk sending her into Canaris' hands. For her contact, a man named Waldoff, may have been given up by Teichmann. From England, there was simply no way of knowing.

They had decided to activate Eva anyway. Their options had been limited; and time was trickling away. When spring came, so would the invasion. But they would send another agent into Germany, to lend her a helping hand. And if Eva could get her information from Klinger, then they would sweep her out, right under Canaris' nose.

Oldfield, of course, had not wanted to make Hobbs the second agent.

His reasoning had been persuasive. He had produced several photographs of Hobbs and Eva together, taken during their long courtship around London. If MI6 had the photographs, Oldfield had said, then the Nazis might have similar ones. It was entirely possible that they would make the connection between Hobbs and Eva, and his attempts to reach her would be frustrated.

Hobbs had argued back with convincing reasons of his own. He had already been established as a traitor in the eyes of Hagen. He could suggest a kidnapping, saying that he was ready to go over to the other side for good. The method of getting into Germany, therefore, would be taken care of. Once he had arrived, Oldfield would wait for four weeks after receiving the letter, to give Hobbs time to emancipate himself, and would then activate Eva. The extraction would be confirmed via a radio message sent by Gehl. Hobbs would make contact. And then they would disappear—riding off together into the sunset, the way he had pictured it, like the heroes at the end of a Hollywood flick.

The argument had gone back and forth. It would be less risky, Oldfield had insisted, to use another agent. To parachute him in. To keep the personal and the professional separated.

Hobbs had countered that Eva would be less likely to trust a stranger who showed up on her doorstep. Hobbs, on the other hand, she knew. Hobbs, she trusted.

Oldfield had raised his eyebrows. *Does she trust you, William?*

He had convinced the man that she did.

But now he felt less certain. Why, after all, *should* she have trusted him? He had used her—seduced her, recruited her, and sent her away.

He quirked his lips sourly. There was no use in thinking it to death.

It was time to go.

But he looked out the window for yet another moment, dallying. The Gehl family was in Wilmersdorf, not so far from this very spot. But Hobbs had no papers, no weapon except the knife with which he had killed Borg. So the journey tonight promised to be dangerous. He was not anxious to undertake it. But he was even less anxious to stay here with Borg.

Nothing to be gained by wasting more time, he thought. The sun had vanished completely now. The stars had come out, glittering like diamonds.

He crossed the room for a final time, stepped gingerly over Borg, and removed his trench coat from the closet. He took a last moment to bolster his faltering courage, and went.

As soon as he was in the street, a strange thing happened: He considered stopping into a beer hall for a drink.

The idea was ludicrous. He did not even have false papers with which to protect himself. But as he walked, surrounded by jovial Berliners, keeping one eye peeled for a taxi, the idea gained a certain mad appeal. He had not had a drink for weeks. He was not accustomed to going weeks without a drink. One drink—what could it hurt?

He heard Oldfield speaking, from somewhere deep in the recesses of memory:

Agents may go days, weeks, months, or even years in complete or near-complete isolation. It is not uncommon for agents in such a situation to feel strange, self-destructive tendencies. Our business is based on deception, and the human mind does not take kindly to that. There is nothing wrong with feeling the urge to confess everything to the nearest friendly ear. But there is something very much wrong, of course, with acting on that impulse.

Was that the urge he felt now—to find some innocent German in some bar and confess everything? He supposed it was. He had committed a murder, after all. He had taken a man's life. He had crossed a line. The need to confess was strong.

Or perhaps he only wanted a drink.

You think too much, he thought.

Stop thinking. Keep moving.

He kept moving.

The people around him were loud, boisterous, drunk. During the days, they walked on eggshells, these Germans. Would the war come, as it seemed it must? Or would the English, at the last possible instant, sue for peace? At night, their tension was released; they drank, danced, brawled, and celebrated as if the world itself was ending. The beer halls and cafés were doing a thriving business behind their new blackout shades.

Litter crackled under his feet as he walked—discarded newspaper, windswept trash, an occasional crumpled leaflet. The British confetti campaign had begun on the very day that war had been declared. Thirteen tons of propaganda had landed in Germany on that first night alone. Hobbs and Borg had watched later deluges together from the apartment window. At one point, Borg had brought a leaflet up to the flat, and they'd shared a laugh over it. The rhetoric was simple and to the point. *Your rulers have condemned you to the massacres, miseries, and privations of a war they cannot ever hope to win.*

A taxi was drifting toward him. He raised a hand and it immediately pulled over to the curb. He slid into the backseat and opened his mouth to state his destination—

—and then paused.

An idea had just occurred to him.

He would go to Eva's flat right now, at this very moment. He knew her address. He would go to her and make his plea, demanding that she give him another chance. He had been rehearsing the words over and over in his mind, during his time locked in the apartment with Borg. It would be a relief to finally say them.

But it would be better, no doubt, to stick to the plan. To visit his contact family in Wilmersdorf, get set up with false papers, and arrange the extraction. In the long run, it would improve his chances—both his and Eva's.

Best to stick with the plan, he thought again. He was far enough behind schedule that another twenty-four hours wouldn't make much of a difference. He would go to Wilmersdorf tonight, and visit Eva tomorrow.

The words he wanted to say to her would still be there tomorrow.

"Hohenzollerndamm," he told the driver blithely. "Wilmersdorf."

LAKE WANNSEE

The staff car drifted to a stop in front of the villa; a single passenger emerged from the backseat.

He was a slender man, lithe and compact, with a widow's peak just beginning to gray around the temples. His hooded, restless eyes promptly scanned the entire area—lake, trees, porch, bristly frost-speckled lawn—in one long, smooth sweep.

The man's name was Frick, and his eyes had not been so rest-less a few months before. But since then he had spent time in Poland as commander of an *Einsatzgruppen* squad, following behind the regular army and rounding up Jews for deportation to the ghetto, and now his eyes never stopped moving.

He was not in the field anymore, however, and there was nothing here at the villa that seemed to merit such extreme cau-tion. After a moment, he made himself relax. The transition from the field to the bureaucracy was not an easy one to make. But he was back in Germany now, and so his role as *Einsatzgruppe* leader needed to be put aside. It was time to don again the mantle he had worn for so many years before—*Kriminal Inspektor* of the Gestapo, and agent of the SD.

Yet the mantle did not fit quite as well as it once had. Frick had seen things in the field, and done things in the field, that had forever changed his nature. The old role felt awkward, too small, as if he had outgrown it. The laws of National Socialism were big and brave and new, and the old ideas, the old ways of doing things, had little place today.

After a few moments, he gave his head a shake and moved out of the sunshine. Once inside the villa, he paused to straighten the cuffs of his shirt and square his jacket's shoulders. Then he pro-ceeded down the shadowed hall until he reached Hagen's office. The door was ajar. He presented himself with a stiff-armed salute.

"*Herr Hagen,*" he said. "*Heil Hitler!*"

Hagen looked up from his desk.

"*Herr Inspektor,*" he said, leaning back in his chair. "Come in. Let me have a look at you."

Frick entered the office. He stood proudly under Hagen's gaze, thinking that the experience he had picked up in the field must show in his bearing. And Hagen, looking him over, seemed impressed.

"You look well," he said at last. "Have a seat, *Herr Inspektor.* We have much to discuss."

Frick took a seat. Hagen opened a silver cigarette case and offered it across the desk. Frick shook his head. From elsewhere in the villa came a soft trickle of music: the "Beer Barrel Polka" by Will Glahe, cheery and somehow surreal.

Hagen took a cigarette for himself, shook off Frick's silver lighter as he held it forward—Frick, who had no taste for tobacco, had found other uses for the lighter on the front—struck a match, and began to speak.

He spoke with oratorical grandness, like a man, Frick thought, who had grown overly accustomed to making speeches. Six years ago, Hagen said, they had planted Frick in the Gestapo as an undercover agent. Frick's purpose there had been to report back to Hagen on Gestapo Chief Müller's machinations, to keep the SD's secret security files up to date. The Sicherheitsdienst, which had been formed in 1932 for the purpose of ferreting out disloyalty within the Nazi organization, had since expanded their purview, becoming the intelligence arm of the secret police. But their original purpose had been to spy on other German spies, and they continued to give this duty top priority.

Frick had done better at the Gestapo, Hagen was saying now, than anyone had assumed he would, rising quickly to the position of *Kriminal Inspektor.* Now that he had returned from the front, it was time to take advantage of this development. Hagen would like to see him begin to assemble his own network of men within the Gestapo, right under Müller's nose. A logical first step . . .

Frick tried to listen, but his mind kept wandering. The cozy warmth of the office, the sound of the radio, and Hagen's lulling monotone conspired to remove him from the here and now. In Poland he had overseen the disposal of a half-dozen difficult Jews. He had forced the women to dig the ditch into which they had then been executed. The experience had been unlike anything else in his life.

It would be difficult, very difficult indeed, to return to the bureaucratic ways of life back in Germany.

But perhaps Hagen realized this. The direction he was leading, Frick came to understand, was intended to liberate Frick from his original duties. Hagen had something else in mind for him.

Presently Hagen finished outlining his plan for placing SD agents, under Frick's supervision, in low-ranking positions throughout the Gestapo. He paused, stabbed out his cigarette, shifted some papers on his desk, and then said:

"It must have been glorious . . . your time spent in the field."

Frick brightened. "Unlike anything I've experienced in my life, Herr Hagen."

"I envy you, *Herr Inspektor.* I've spent too much time behind this desk. Far too much time."

Frick, who secretly agreed, only shrugged. "Somebody must make the sacrifice."

"Indeed," Hagen said. He thought for a moment, then blinked. "In any case," he said, "I have an opportunity for you, if you are interested. It would enable you to avoid a return to such drudgery. And it would take advantage of your connections with the Gestapo. You are uniquely qualified, I would venture, for this operation . . . if you are interested."

Frick leaned forward. "Go on," he said.

41

"There is a man—an Engländer—who was used by this office as an asset. A traitor who had experience with MI6. You may remember him. William Hobbs."

Frick shrugged again. Most of his memories from before his time in Poland were washed-out, sepia-toned. "Perhaps," he said.

"He came to Germany nearly five months ago. When the debriefing was finished, he was informed that he must stay in Berlin for the foreseeable future. This seems not to have agreed with him." Hagen paused. "I received word this morning," he said carefully, "that Hobbs has murdered his case officer—an unfortunate fellow named Borg—and vanished. Borg's corpse was found in the apartment they shared on Leipziger Strasse. His throat had been slit."

Frick nodded, blank-faced.

"Hobbs cannot have gotten far, of course. No doubt he's still in Berlin, in hiding somewhere. Yet until now we have not been able to track him down. It makes me suspect that perhaps he was not truly a traitor, *Herr Inspektor.* It makes me suspect that he had planned for this eventuality."

"I see."

"Perhaps MI6 arranged all this in advance—his treachery, the kidnapping—on the assumption that we would not allow him to leave. If that is the case, I'm afraid we have been outmaneuvered. He has been successfully planted in Germany."

Frick thinned his lips. He would not have put it past the shrewd, conniving British. They had been practicing the game of espionage for centuries upon centuries, and had become masters at it.

"I want this man back in my custody," Hagen said. "He must have a contact here in Berlin—someone who is sheltering him."

"Of course."

"I would very much like you to find him for me."

"Of course," Frick said again.

Hagen reached into the drawer of his desk and withdrew a file. He passed it over. "William Hobbs," he repeated. "Do not hesitate to come to me with any questions you may have. And move quickly. I would prefer to have him alive—but I would settle for having him."

"I understand, Herr Hagen."

Hagen looked at him for another moment. Something in his face softened. "Tell me," he said then. "I have heard reports about the conduct of the *Einsatzgruppen*. They have taken matters into their own hands, I have been told, on the Polish front. It makes the Christians very nervous."

Frick smiled.

"It is a new age, Herr Hagen. New methods are required to produce results."

"How I envy you," Hagen said wistfully.

"Perhaps next time you can join me. When we move West."

"Perhaps," Hagen said. "Perhaps." His eyes turned momentarily inward, then sharpened again. He stood. "Have a look at the file," he said. "Keep me informed."

Frick stood opposite him. "I will have results shortly."

"I trust you will."

"*Heil Hitler*," Frick said.

"*Heil Hitler*," Hagen answered. "And *Herr Inspektor*— welcome home."

43

Chapter Three

CHARLOTTENBURG, BERLIN

The More You Work The Better Sleep You Need, Eva Bernhardt read. *Make a nightcup of Bourn-Vita a regular habit—it will soothe you, help digestion and calm your whole body.*

Eva, slumped over her desk with her chin propped in one hand, had to read the advertisement twice to get the sense from it. Good sleep was not something with which she had been intimately acquainted in recent nights. But now would be no time to slack off at work and risk drawing attention. No, everything must continue by the usual routine.

The usual routine, in its dull and quiet way, was torturous.

She took lunch alone at her desk: cold red cabbage with vinegar and boiled potatoes. The meal did not sit well in her stomach. For the rest of the day, she felt vaguely, insistently nauseous.

Afternoon turned on its sleepy axis; she felt herself nodding. She sat up straight, pinched the soft flesh inside her forearm, and tried to concentrate. Her work—supplying ammunition for the radio propagandists based in the Rundfunk—involved divining profound things from seemingly innocuous materials smuggled out of England. The work was tedious, and often absurd. But Propaganda Minister Goebbels, who rarely hesitated to invent outlandish claims for his broadcasts, liked to spice his lies with an occasional fact—so her position continued to exist, regardless of the quality of her results.

Mrs. Brown has organized a gardening corps. At the end of a hard day she goes home to tea and a good wash with Knight's Castile soap. The kindly luxurious lather of Knight's Castile soothes away that feeling of exhaustion, tones up the skin and keeps the complexion youthfully clear. . . .

A shadow fell across her desk. When Eva looked up, she saw Gretl Koch smiling down at her.

"You look tired," Gretl said.

Eva returned the smile as best she could. Gretl was one of the nicer girls at the Rundfunk—a social butterfly, with no lack of wealthy older boyfriends.

"What you need," Gretl went on, "is some fun. My friend Joseph made a killing last week. Some big naval contract. Tonight he wants to splurge. We're going dancing."

Eva felt a tug of envy. Even before she had found herself in her current situation, she had not been the type to go out dancing.

She had always been the outsider, the girl who ended up waiting in vain to be asked for a turn on the floor.

"Come with us," Gretl said. "It'll do you good."

"That's nice of you," Eva said. "I can't tonight. Next time?"

"Now, why does that sound so familiar?"

"I appreciate the offer, Gretl."

"He's got a brother. We could give him a ring, and all do the town together."

"Next time," Eva promised.

"You know," Gretl said gloomily, "you're not getting any younger." But she said it with a grin, and then left Eva alone, her skirt swishing busily as she moved back to her own desk.

By half past four, Eva had reached the end of her rope. Two advertisements for menstrual aids were spread on her desk, one for A-K tablets ("war will not wait on any woman's weakness") and one for Rendells Feminine Hygiene ("a product of intimate importance"). She sighed heavily and set down her pen. Her brain was hardly working anymore. Her stomach felt turgid and sour.

It was time to go home.

She had just finished her bath and was regarding herself desultorily in the mirror above the sink—there were wrinkles around her eyes and her mouth; when had those appeared?— when the rapping came on her door.

The rapping was steady and insistent, the kind of sound that might attract the wrong sort of attention from the neighbors. Eva pushed down the first feathery stirrings of panic and rushed to answer it quickly.

She was wearing a loose robe; as she crossed the tiny basement apartment she held it tightly closed against her breast. She
reached the door and then wavered before opening it. It was past
nine, and she was not expecting a visitor. It could not be good
news. If the Gestapo were to come for her, in fact, this was how it
might happen. For a moment, she considered not answering the
door at all. She considered going into the bedroom, pulling the
blankets up above her head, and waiting to be left alone—as if
that childish trick might actually have a chance of thwarting the
Gestapo.

Then the rapping started again. She swallowed once, with a
click. Her fingers moved smoothly over the three locks on the
door, worked the mechanisms, dropped to the knob and twisted it.

Klinger was there, his eyes sparkling with dark mirth. "Surprise!" he crowed.

He staggered past her with the smell of schnapps following
in a thick cloud. Once inside the flat, he paused, swayed, and
turned.

"You," he said. His finger wagged in her face. "You . . ."

Eva waited.

"You . . . must have been . . . a beautiful . . . baby . . ."

He turned away, singing louder. "You must have been . . .
a beautiful . . . girl . . ."

She shut the door, took a moment to compose her face, and
then followed him into the apartment. He had moved to the wireless radio on the bookshelf. Now he switched it on and began to
tune through the stations.

After looking at Klinger's back for a few seconds, Eva went to
put on a kettle, wondering if any of the neighbors had seen him.
What did he expect from her tonight? He had probably gotten

drunk and then started feeling romantic. But he seemed more interested in the radio, for the moment, than in her.

He settled on a broadcast by Lord Haw-Haw. Lord Haw-Haw was in unusually good form, his nasal voice describing Germany's good intentions toward a pacifistic Britain with an unmistakable sneer. Klinger listened for a moment, his head bent, his eyes closed. "Feh," he said then. He switched off the radio, moved to the threadbare sofa, and collapsed onto it heavily.

Eva left the kettle to boil and went back into the living room. "Otto," she said. "You shouldn't be here."

His eyes had closed again. He was nodding rhythmically, as if following some tune playing in his head.

"It's late," she said gently. "You ought to go home."

"My wife's at home," he said. His eyes opened. "Did you know I have a wife, *Liebling*?"

She shook her head.

"Well, it's true. A wonderful woman, my wife. You should meet her sometime. You have something in common, you know. Me." He shook his head, then began to sing again. *"I married an angel . . ."*

The kettle whistled. Eva returned to the kitchen, found two cups, set them on a tray beside a teapot, and went to join Klinger on the couch.

But Klinger was back before the bookcase. His finger traveled unsteadily over the spines. It paused before a book Eva had never read: *Deutsche Mathematik.* The book was only for show. She had long since purged her collection of anything that might be considered suspicious reading material, filling it instead with books that had been sanctioned by the propaganda ministry.

Klinger took down the book and began to page through it.

49

"Ah!" he said. "Look here—listen. 'The proposition that mathematics can be considered without a racial perspective'"— the words came out slurred: *The proposhition that mathematics can be conshidered without a racial pershpective*—"'carries within itself the germs of destruction of German science.'"

Eva set down the tray in her hands, and made no comment.

"Huh," Klinger said thickly. He returned to the couch, shaking the book in his hand. "Do you know," he asked, "that my father was once an honored professor at the University of Berlin?"

She sat beside him, poured the tea. "No," she said. "I didn't know that."

"Of course not. Why would you? I've taken great pains, little one, to keep it a secret. If you look at the official records, in fact, you'd discover that my father is not my father at all." He laughed—a brittle laugh. "I'm a simple man, dear Eva. A simple man with simple tastes. Why should I invite trouble?"

She shook her head helplessly.

"Feh," Klinger said. "I know what some might say to that. He is your father; you are his son. You have a duty, Otto—that's what they would say. But we are very different, my father and I. He cared for ideas, Eva." He looked at her with sudden intensity. *"Ideas."*

She reached for a cup of tea and pressed it into his hands. He set it down again immediately.

"When it came time to join the Teachers' League, my father refused. He wouldn't take the oath. Wouldn't even hear of it. Do you know the oath? All teachers were forced to take it, from the lowest kindergarten to the highest university. 'To be loyal and obedient to Adolf Hitler.' Well, he wouldn't have it. *Racial science*, indeed. Feh. Centuries of learning . . . out the window. He wouldn't have it."

His voice was climbing now, in volume and in timbre.

"He was a man of ideas, my father. And he paid the price. So I am not his son! I am the son of some other Herr Klinger, if you read my official records. A farmer from the east. Why should I invite that sort of scrutiny, that my father's son would have to face?"

"Otto . . ."

"I don't need that. Dear, darling Eva. Would you blame me—"

"Keep your voice down," she said.

He trailed off, then looked at her cannily.

"Yes," he said after a moment. "We wouldn't want to attract attention to ourselves, would we?"

That same dark humor danced in his eyes, feverishly.

"Not us," he said. "A traitor and a spy."

Cool shock took Eva, chilling her, making her stomach twist.

Klinger raised the cup again, drank, ran the back of his hand over his lips, and belched. "Don't look that way," he said. "I'm only joking. Dear, darling Eva."

She looked away.

"You're no spy, of course. You're only the latest in a long string of beautiful women to throw themselves at me. Why, it happens every day. Several times a day. My tremendous natural charm." He laughed. "Why should I suspect that you have any ulterior motive? That would be foolish of me. Worse than foolish. Paranoid. Eh?"

She reached for her tea. Her hand was shaking. She steadied it with her other hand and forced herself to bring the cup to her mouth.

51

"So nervous!" he said wonderingly.

When she spoke again, her voice was thin. "Otto, you shouldn't say things like that."

"Feh," he said.

"It's dangerous to say things like that."

"Feh."

"You're drunk. You should go home. To your wife."

He sat in silence, glowering. Emotions played across his face transparently, as they do on the faces of drunks and children. Then he murmured something, seemingly to himself. It sounded like *"Schlieffen."*

She leaned closer. "Did you . . . say something?"

His eyes closed again, squeezed tight, then opened.

"Nothing," he said. "You're right. I'm drunk." He looked at her searchingly, and stood. "Forgive me, Eva. I'm sorry."

"Go home, Otto. Go to bed."

She had the sense he was on the verge of adding something else; but then he turned away. "Good night," he said simply, and moved to the door.

He began to try to work the bolts there. Astoundingly, he got them open. Then he turned again, and said, without meeting her eyes, "They will know."

As quickly as he had appeared, he was gone.

She looked after him for what seemed like a very long time. Finally, she stood, moved to the door herself, and shot the bolts. She hugged herself tightly, leaning against the thin wood and shivering.

A traitor and a spy.

Had she betrayed herself?

She ran back over the conversation in her mind. No, she

decided, she had not betrayed herself. He had been testing her, perhaps—and she had not betrayed herself. But nor had she taken advantage of the opportunity. He had confessed about his wife, even about his father. It would have been a fine chance to suggest something, to make some inroads toward her ultimate goal. But she had let the chance pass.

She let out a long, shuddering sigh. The temptation to burrow into bed returned. In bed nothing could get to her. Ridiculous, of course; but a soothing thought nevertheless.

She peeled off her robe, trailing it across the floor, and crawled into bed without even brushing her teeth. She felt suddenly exhausted.

She was not cut out for this. It had started as a game—years before, miles away. But now it was no game.

A traitor and a spy.

They will know.

Who would know? The Nazis? Did they suspect him? Were they watching her?

The old temptation returned, to blame Hobbs. If Hobbs had been a more honorable man—if Hobbs had not misrepresented himself to her from the very beginning—she would not have found herself in this position. Then the old rejoinder: she had made the choice herself; she had followed a higher purpose. She was doing the right thing, for the right reasons.

But she had been so young when she had agreed to it—only twenty. Was it fair for a girl of twenty to make decisions that would affect the rest of her life?

She doused the lamp. One came to important junctures without even realizing at the time, she thought, just how important they were. If she had stayed on her parents' farm in Saxony, she would be living a simple life today. Riding horses, cooking, and probably married by now. She would have her own family; simple pleasures. But she had been anxious to leave the farm, to study in England—to do something more with her life.

She only wished she'd realized at the time what she was getting herself into.

She closed her eyes. Were all spies so confused? It seemed unlikely.

Schlieffen.

They will know.

Her eyes opened.

Not the Nazis, she thought. The British, Klinger had meant. The British would know. *Schlieffen.* He had told her something. But what?

She would have to find out. She would have to see him again.

A traitor and a spy.

Sleep, that night, was a long time coming.

PRINZ ALBRECHT STRASSE

Herr *Kriminal Inspektor*," Hauptmann said. "Have you got a moment?"

Frick glanced up. Hauptmann was standing in the doorway, holding a thin sheaf of papers under one arm. He hoped, no doubt, to add the papers to the already formidable pile sitting on Frick's desk.

"Not if those are for me," Frick said.

Hauptmann smiled, and came farther into the office. He was a stocky man with coarse chestnut hair and an offbeat sense of humor that was well known around Gestapo headquarters. "Too much paperwork, *Herr Inspektor?*"

"Far too much, Hauptmann. Far too much."

"I seem to remember that you used to be fond of paperwork—before your time spent in the field."

Frick frowned. To the best of his recollection, he had never been particularly fond of paperwork. But then, he always had been fond of organization. And his powers of recollection had faltered since his return from the front. He had more and more trouble, these days, keeping his mind focused.

Or perhaps it was just Hauptmann's idea of a joke.

Hauptmann waved the papers in his hand. "You'll want to take a look at this," he said. "It might cheer you up."

"What is it?"

"A report, *Herr Inspektor,* from a *Blockwart* in Wilmersdorf. I'd be glad to follow it up myself, if you like, this very evening."

Hauptmann was glowing with barely contained self-satisfaction. The workday was already finished; the man's offer to follow up himself seemed strange. Frick held out his hand.

"If I need you, *Herr Kriminal Assistant*, I'll find you."

Hauptmann looked pained. It must have been a promising report indeed, Frick thought, if the man was so eager to track it down. Hauptmann relinquished the papers, turned, and then paused at the door and turned back. "Got a joke for you," he said. "Two Luftwaffe pilots walk into a bar. And who do they see sitting there but Field Marshall Goering himself? Goering has a plate in front of him. Pork schnitzel, smoked salmon, pheasant, venison. One pilot turns to the other—"

"*Herr Kriminal Assistant*," Frick said.

"Yes?"

"My schedule is very full today."

Hauptmann straightened.

"Of course, *Herr Inspektor*," he said, and let himself out.

Frick looked after the man for a moment, then turned his attention to the papers on his desk.

He soon realized that the *Kriminal Assistant*'s eagerness had not been misplaced. Hauptmann had been lending a hand with the search for William Hobbs, and it seemed that he had struck gold. The papers described a family named Gehl, residents of the suburb of Wilmersdorf. Three days before, a mysterious visitor had appeared on the Gehls' doorstep. Several neighbors had immediately reported the man's appearance to the block supervisor. He was a tall man, they said, with an athlete's build, who moved with a slight limp. Since his arrival, he had been seen slipping out several times, always under cover of darkness, only to return within an hour.

The Gehl family—wife Ursula, husband Ernst—worked in the import-export business, and thanks to the nature of their transactions they had maintained ties with the British until fairly recently. It was not beyond the realm of possibility, the *Blockwart* suggested in his report, that the Gehl family might be British sympathizers. It was therefore not beyond the realm of possibility that this strange visitor might actually be somebody of considerable interest, a refugee or a spy. The report ended with a proposal that the Gestapo pay a visit to the Gehl family and demand to see the visitor's papers.

Frick read the report twice, then set it aside. Over the past few days, his men had chased down a half-dozen leads concerning Hobbs, and had found nothing except dead ends. But none of the other leads had seemed half so promising.

The desk work was suffocating him. He decided to follow up on this one personally.

He was just preparing to stand when he caught the odor of fresh bread, wafting through the air of the office like a half-remembered melody.

Frick paused. It was his mother's bread, he realized; the kind she had made on Sunday afternoons, the kind that filled the house with hearty good smells promising heavy dinners and early bed-times. His mother's bread—here in the offices of the Gestapo.

Very strange, he thought.

As he sat, smelling the ghost scent of his mother's fresh bread, his mind began to wander. It wandered back to the front. The sky was cemetery gray, with twin columns of dun-colored smoke rising from the scarred ground. A young Jewess was touching her heart, almost tenderly, looking him straight in the eye. "Eighteen," she said. It was her age, he understood. She wanted him to know how old she was before he shot her. "Eighteen," she said again, with her hand on her chest, as if that might somehow save her life.

Then his finger had tightened on the trigger . . .

A telephone was ringing.

Frick snapped back to the present, reaching for the phone on his desk. He had it to his ear before he realized that it had been some other telephone ringing, in some other office. He set it down again.

For a moment, his mind was perfectly blank.

Then his thoughts turned slowly, inexorably, back to the girl.

She had been a beautiful girl: dark-eyed, raven-haired. "Eigh-teen," she had said. Half-plaintive, half-accusatory. "Eighteen."

When he came back to reality again, the office was dark. Light from the hallway leaked stealthily under the door.

He sat up straighter. The smell of bread was dissipating now.

What had he been thinking, before his mind had wandered? He couldn't recall.

His eyes ticked over the contents of the desk: the file, the telephone, the framed photograph of his mother, the blotter, the pencil. Ordinary things. Nothing of importance there. But he had the nagging feeling that he had been thinking of something important, before his mind had taken him back to the front. Hadn't he?

He licked his lips, then shook his head. He needed a good night's sleep. That was all.

He would remember in the morning.

He let himself out, leaving the file untouched on the edge of his desk.

Chapter Four

HOHENZOLLERNDAMM, WILMERSDORF

Once Wilmersdorf had been a bourgeois district.

Then, at the turn of the century, the immigrants had come. The old Junker mansions had been split into apartments to accommodate the influx; the neighborhood had turned plainly residential. Now the few opulent manors in the area were separated by tenements, with a profusion of bulbous blue church domes—the architecture of the Russian Orthodoxy—rising above the rooftops.

William Hobbs looked out at the neighborhood for a

moment, then let the curtain fall closed. When he turned from the window, he was surprised to see Ernst Gehl standing by the grandfather clock, watching him.

"Herr Gehl," he said. "You startled me."

Gehl gave a listless smile. He was a tall, distinguished-looking man in his late sixties. Something about him reminded Hobbs of Arturo Toscanini, the legendary conductor: a resemblance through the nose and the eyes, in the high forehead and the saturnine demeanor.

Gehl turned to the towering grandfather clock, opened it, and began to adjust the weights inside. "Going out again?" he asked.

"For the last time," Hobbs said.

Gehl did not turn to face him, but Hobbs could read the man's thoughts as clearly as if he'd spoken them aloud. Every time Hobbs left the modest brick house, he risked bringing attention to the Gehls. In one way, Herr Gehl would have preferred that he stayed locked in the attic, out of sight and out of mind. On the other hand, Herr Gehl knew that Hobbs could not move on—to the extraction site, away from the Gehl house for good—until he had successfully contacted the agent for whom he had come here.

"I won't be coming back," Hobbs said.

Gehl, still occupied with the clock, gave a negligent wave. Hobbs, of course, had already left the house three times hoping to make contact. Gehl did not have any reason to believe that this time would be different.

Hobbs looked at the man's back for another moment. He felt a slow, rising surge of sympathy. Ernst Gehl and his wife, Ursula, Hobbs knew, were reluctant associates of the British. They had promised their help in the days when it had been easy to promise such help, when noble virtues had seemed most important, when the specter of war had been something on the distant horizon. Now war had come and eyes were everywhere. Gehl and his wife were already guilty of treason, so they could hardly turn back; but they plainly regretted the position in which they found themselves.

After watching Gehl adjust the clock for a few moments, he turned to the staircase and climbed to the house's second floor. Apologies and thanks would be worthless. The best thing he could do for them would be to get on with his mission, and out of their lives.

A heavy chain hung from a trapdoor in the second-story ceiling. When he pulled on it, a ladder folded open like an oversized accordion. He moved up the rungs, into the close confines of the attic. He had spent the past few days living in this attic—but it had come, in that short span of time, to feel something like home.

Which was, he thought now, really rather sad.

He came off the top rung and turned to the small crate that he had been using as a desk. He lit the paraffin lamp atop the crate and then picked up the envelope sitting beside it. He held the envelope for a moment, fighting the temptation to open it, to make certain he had gotten the words right. He had already been over the letter countless times; the words were as right as he could make them.

He replaced the envelope on the crate, then turned to his small collection of supplies and began to organize them for his departure.

The supplies, for the most part, had come from the Gehls. Hobbs fastened the leather holster to his ankle and then slipped the silenced 9mm Beretta inside. He checked his papers—

identity card, ration card, work permit—and found them satis-
factory. He located the keys to the Talta—the Gehls' car, which
they had offered for his use. They must have been desperate to get
rid of him indeed, he thought, to give up a car in such difficult
times. But what else was new? Everywhere he had ever gone in his
life, he had brought unpleasantness along with him. Everywhere
he had ever been, they had been anxious for him to leave.

After pocketing the keys, he shrugged on his trench coat. He
put the letter in one pocket and then reached into the other, his
fingers brushing past his last pack of cigarettes, to the mustache.
He had made the mustache himself, from cotton balls in the
Gehls' medicine cabinet. He removed it, licked the back—the
adhesive had come from an envelope—and then patted it onto his
upper lip, over his own slim mustache.

He stood for a moment, in the flickering light of the paraffin
lamp, feeling faintly ridiculous.

Too many disguises, he thought. Too many years of playing
roles. The lines blurred when one played a role for too many
years.

Perhaps, beneath all the various disguises, the real William
Hobbs no longer existed. Or perhaps the real William Hobbs had
never truly existed at all. Before becoming a patriot, after all, he
had played a variety of roles: pacifist, nonconformist, socialist,
Fascist; anything that would give him access to a warm meeting
hall, a sense of community and purpose. For all his life he had
been trying on different masks, one after another. Who was to say
if there was any face at all, below the masquerades?

Then he thought of Eva.

When he had been with Eva, he had not been playing a role.
When he had been with Eva, he had only been himself.

And he had let her slip through his fingers: like so many grains of sand.

After thinking for a moment, he began to move again. His hands took inventory, checking the letter, the keys, the papers, the gun. They were all in order. He was ready. He had discovered during his excursions that most nights after dinner, Eva went for a walk. He planned to orchestrate a meeting during her evening stroll. He would press the letter into her hands and hope that the men watching her didn't catch on. It was not the most brilliant plan in the world, but then, he was not the most brilliant man in the world. Besides, simplicity was effective.

He paused, cocking his head. *Simplicity is effective.*

Had that been Oldfield's?

Or had it come from further back? From childhood? Perhaps from his father?

He couldn't remember.

From Oldfield, he thought. His father had never taught him anything worth remembering. He had been too busy drinking himself to death.

His hat was resting on the bare mattress. He picked it up, put it on his head, and took a moment to say farewell to his temporary home. Then he found the cane leaning against one wall, doused the lamp, and went downstairs again.

He parked the Talta three blocks from Eva's flat.

As he walked, he felt the gun pressing against his ankle. It was a reassuring pressure, giving him a feeling of security. He had not forgotten the sensation of slitting Borg's throat. It was not a sensation he was eager to repeat. The gun, however, was impersonal.

He could use it, if he had to, without hesitation. Even better would be a rifle. He had spent many a day during his youth duck hunting in the fens outside of Surrey. With a rifle in his hands, he would feel almost invincible. . . .

But for now he was satisfied with the Beretta. It was a silenced version of the standard Italian service pistol used by OVRA, the Italian secret police; the holster had been modified to accept both gun and silencer as a single unit.

When he was within a block of Eva's apartment, he leaned against a wall, situating himself so that he was invisible to both watchers. They could not see him, and he could not see them. But he would see Eva, if she followed the route she had followed before—when she reached the corner, before turning to continue around the block.

He waited, smoking. A light drizzle picked up, sprinkled cool rain, and dissipated.

Fifteen minutes passed. He began to feel anxious. Perhaps she would not take her walk at all tonight. Then where would he be? He would need to return to the Gehls' house, to wait for another chance. But he had told the Gehls he was not coming back.

He lit another cigarette, and held his ground.

A few minutes later, he saw a Gestapo agent moving down the street. He reached for his cane and prepared to move. He would take a stroll around the block himself, and would take the chance, therefore, of missing Eva. But if there was a better option, he couldn't see it.

He was just taking his first step when the Gestapo agent found another man to occupy his attention: a short, swarthy fellow weaving drunkenly down the sidewalk. Hobbs checked himself, watching.

The men were out of earshot, but he could guess the conversation easily enough. The Gestapo agent was requesting papers. The swarthy fellow patted himself down, found them, and offered them. They were evidently not enough to satisfy the Gestapo man, who then extended an offer to come into *Schutzhaft,* or protective custody. It was not an invitation that could be refused.

"*Macht mit der Hacken,*" the man ordered loudly: Make with the heels.

Hobbs looked away as they moved past.

After another five minutes, he saw Eva, walking quickly with her head down, wearing her snood and her plain winter coat. He licked his lips, tossed the cigarette aside, planted the cane, and began to shuffle toward her.

The mustache felt lopsided. Too late to fiddle with it now; he had come into view of the watchers. He kept walking, trying not to overact his role, using the cane sparingly.

Eva looked distracted. As they drew near to each other, she glanced up. Her eyes landed on his face without a spark of recognition. She looked down again, stepping to one side so they could pass each other. Hobbs waited—and waited—and then misplaced the cane, stumbling into her. At the same time, his free hand dipped into his pocket, withdrawing the letter.

"Oh!" she said. "Pardon me."

He leaned his full weight against her—an old man who had lost his balance. Her hands moved reflexively to support him. "*Danke,*" he mumbled, and pressed the letter against her side.

She looked down at it, frowning.

"Take it," he hissed.

She took the letter.

Then Hobbs was moving away, not looking back. He resisted the temptation to sneak a glance at the watchers. He forced himself to move slowly, evenly.

She had not recognized him.

He had thought that she would recognize him, once they were close to each other. But there had been nothing in her eyes except startled irritation. It made him feel disappointed. Was he so far from her mind, these days?

He kept walking. Now he risked a peek over his shoulder. The man in the doorway was still in the doorway—but watching him. He quickly turned his eyes back to the sidewalk. He was drawing near to the newspaper and book stand. The urge to hurry was strong. He bit it down.

Her face had looked older, wearier. Yet more beautiful than ever, in its ordinary way. The features had been more clearly defined. She was not a girl any longer. She had come into her own.

Then he was passing the newspaper stand. The man behind the counter was staring at him balefully. In the next moment, he was raising a hand, giving a signal to the one in the doorway.

Hobbs moved faster.

After another ten paces, he had reached the far corner of the block. Before turning, he glanced back over his shoulder. The man in the newspaper stand was pointing at him. The other was hurrying forward, hands in pockets. Eva was still moving away, continuing her walk as if nothing out of the ordinary had happened.

He stepped around the corner and then broke into a run.

A voice rang out, *"Stehenbleiben!"* Stop or I'll shoot.

He kept running, throwing the cane aside.

Halfway down the block, he stepped into a recessed doorway. He bent down and pulled the Beretta from its holster, his heart thudding. He counted to three and then stepped out from the doorway.

The watcher was there—moving cautiously forward, one hand still in his pocket, the other holding a gun. When Hobbs stepped out, he looked almost comically surprised.

Hobbs raised the Beretta and fired three shots into the man's chest: *Fpp fpp fpp.*

Then ran back in the direction from which he'd come. They had seen him passing the letter. The other man, therefore, had to be silenced as well.

The man in the book stand was fishing around beneath a stack of newspapers. Hobbs charged toward him, aiming the gun, straight-armed. He fired once; missed. A magazine hanging from a rack flapped as if taken by a sudden breeze. Then the man had his own gun in his hands. There was a sudden, flat *crack.* A bullet hissed through the air an inch from Hobbs' ear.

He fired again, still moving forward, and again he missed.

The man returned fire. Hobbs felt a strong hand take his leg and push it out from under him. As he fell, he squeezed the trigger twice more. *Fpp fpp.*

When he looked up, the man was nowhere to be seen. But a stain of blood was on the flapping magazine, peppered with off-white shards of bone.

He gained his feet. One hand moved to his leg, searching for the wound. The bullet had entered just above his knee. When he put weight on the leg, it sent a rill of pain straight into his central nervous system, making his teeth clench.

If he could make the car, he still had a chance.

He began to move, dragging the leg. It was the right leg, the one that had given him trouble ever since the rugby injury years before. Ruined, now, beyond any doubt. Well, his rugby days had been finished anyway. He almost laughed at the thought.

For a moment, the pain welled, threatening to take him away. The edges of his field of vision blurred. Then the darkness receded, leaving him on his feet.

A whistle was blowing somewhere. Someone was calling after him. He ignored it.

He reached the corner. Eva was gone. Just as well. She had a better chance without him, now.

Halfway down the next block he became aware of feet pounding behind him. The whistle continued to blow, shrilly. He turned his head and saw two Gestapo agents in pursuit. He raised the Beretta and fired in their general direction, hoping to make them duck for cover. But the hammer clicked impotently on an empty chamber. Of course; the gun used a seven-shot magazine.

One of the Gestapo kept blowing his whistle. The other drew a pistol of his own and took long, careful aim. Hobbs turned again, dropped the empty Beretta, and hurried off.

A bullet hammered into the sidewalk two feet away, sending up a chip of concrete. He ducked. Then he could see the Talta, fifty feet away, impossibly distant.

His vision clouded again. When it cleared he was behind the wheel, somehow. The keys were in his hand, but his hand was slicked with blood. He promptly dropped the keys. When he bent down to retrieve them, the rear windshield blew out. If he hadn't ducked . . .

His fingers skittered over the keys, found slippery purchase. He raised them, jammed them into the ignition, and fired it.

When he looked into the rearview mirror, he saw the two Gestapo directly behind the car: one taking aim again, patiently; the other still blowing his damned whistle.

He threw the car into reverse and jammed his foot down onto the accelerator.

The double thump brought a lunatic grin to his lips.

His hands moved for the gearshift again. The gears gnashed as he tried to find first. Then it had clicked into place; the Talta was lurching forward. A moment later, he was half a block away, gaining speed.

The Gehls, he thought. They would need to extend themselves one final time before they were rid of him. They would need to help him patch the leg, or he would have little chance of making it to the extraction site.

William, he thought. *You bollixed that up, but good.*

But perhaps Eva would still have a chance. If she read the letter . . . if she moved quickly enough . . .

He forced the thought from his mind. Time for it later. But it kept nagging. He had sealed her fate. For the second time in his life, he had put Eva in danger.

His chest felt hollow. His mind was spinning in strange, nightmarish directions. The bullet in his leg. Christ, it hurt.

He pushed it all away. *Focus*, he thought.

He focused. And drove.

Eva heard the shots as she was stepping around the corner farthest from her apartment.

She cocked her head, listening. The letter that the old man had forced on her was clutched tightly inside her pocket. She wondered if the shots had anything to do with the old man. They probably did. She did not know who he was—but she knew he meant trouble.

She was probably minutes from being arrested.

She was probably about to die.

After a moment, she made herself continue walking.

Her fingers worked at the letter in her pocket. She wanted to open and read it right now, right here in the street. Perhaps it would explain something. But there were too many eyes out here. No, the letter needed to wait until she had reached her apartment again.

If she reached her apartment again.

She kept walking, with an effort, at a normal pace. Acting again, she suddenly realized, as she had been at the Hotel Adlon with Klinger. Her role tonight was that of Eva Bernhardt, sleepwalker. Calm, content with her lot, on a simple evening stroll.

Something to do with Klinger, she thought. Something to do with the word he had whispered: *Schlieffen.* Perhaps they had arrested him, and he had confessed telling her the word. But if that was the case, why was she still at liberty? And who was the old man?

She turned the third corner, and headed back toward her apartment.

Halfway down the block, a corpse lay sprawled on the sidewalk.

Three policemen were clustered around the dead man. Eva crossed the street, averting her eyes. How would she have felt, in this situation, had she been innocent? Nervous, focused on herself, trying to avoid becoming involved. She portrayed these feelings in her walk and her demeanor, and none of the men glanced in her direction.

When she turned the last corner, she saw another cluster of policemen, surrounding the little newspaper and book stand across from her building. A few Gestapo agents mingled with them. They were looking down at something inside the stand, speaking in low voices.

She closed the distance to her apartment. Nobody moved to stop her.

She let herself in, descending the four steps, and opened the three locks. Then she was safe inside her own apartment—except that she didn't feel safe. The mask of impassivity dissolved; her face contorted like a child's on the verge of a crying fit.

She took the envelope from her pocket, tore it open, and began to read.

Dearest Eva, the letter began.

She recognized the handwriting immediately: a spiky, nearly illegible scrawl. The old man's face clicked back into her mind's eye. That tremendous, ridiculous white mustache. A fake mustache, she realized suddenly. The hunched posture, the cane; all a disguise.

The old man had been Hobbs.

She turned her eyes back to the letter.

Dearest Eva:
The Abwehr is watching you. You're not safe in Berlin any longer. I've come to help you get out.
An airplane will meet us on 15 March just north of Goth-mund, on the Trave River. A fisherman named Thomas Brandt will shelter you until the extraction. His door on the Fischerweg will have a circle carved into the top right corner. Identify yourself as his cousin. I will meet you there before 15 March.

71

You must complete your mission if possible before going to Gothmund. But if you don't, go anyway. Take care. You cannot let them follow you to the extraction site.
I hope you can find it in your heart to forgive me. I've taken great risks to reach you with this message. I hope you realize that means something.
Good luck.

There was no signature.

She read the letter twice. A laugh started to bubble up behind her lips. If it came out, it would be hysterical. She covered her mouth with one hand. Her heart was accelerating inside her chest. It seemed it would keep accelerating until it had burst. She waited; at last her heart began to slow. The urge to laugh passed. But she kept her hand plastered over her mouth, just to be safe, as she read the letter again.

The Abwehr is watching you.

Then she was swinging over to the other extreme: cool and distant, watching herself from the outside. The threat of laughter was gone. She took her hand from her mouth.

An airplane will meet us on 15 March.

Today was the eleventh. That left only four days.

You must complete your mission if possible before going to Gothmund. But if not, go anyway.

Her mission. To convince Klinger to try to get a look at the OKW files. She had failed at that, if she truly had run out of time. Yet he had given her the one clue: *Schlieffen*. One that might mean more to others than it meant to her. *They will know.*

Until this point, the letter made sense. For she had known,

deep down, that she was being watched. She hadn't confronted the thought consciously—the implications were too disturbing—but deep down she had known.

The last few lines of the letter, however, were confusing.

I hope you can find it in your heart to forgive me.

Hobbs, begging forgiveness? She had never thought she would see the day.

I've taken great risks to reach you with this message. I hope you realize that means something.

She folded the letter.

From outside came the sounds of activity. An ambulance siren. The dead man she had passed during her walk, she thought. Suddenly, she understood: The man had been watching her. Perhaps he had seen Hobbs passing the letter to her. And perhaps Hobbs had killed the man.

If that was the case, a knock might come on the door at any moment.

And this time it wouldn't be Klinger. This time it would be the Abwehr, or the Gestapo.

You're not safe in Berlin any longer.

Those words had been written before the dead man had caused such a commotion outside. Now, she thought, they were doubtless even more true.

She stood for another moment. A euphoric panic was rising inside her. Every moment she stood here, her chances of escaping decreased. She needed to leave. To abandon all of it: her job, her mission, her dull and lonely life. And not to look back.

Why did that thought make her feel euphoric? She had given up on Hobbs long ago. Even if he had changed, she wanted no part of him.

She heard footsteps moving toward the front door of the

building. She tensed. She was too late, even now. They were coming for her.

Then the footsteps were moving past. Someone was laughing. She relaxed, exhaling.

She read the letter one final time and then crumpled it into a ball. Suddenly, that seemed insufficient. She carried it to the sink, found a box of matches beneath the stove, and lit one. When the flame touched the paper, it turned into a tongue, licking greedily.

She dropped the paper into the sink and watched it turn to ash.

Stood for one more moment, thinking.

Then she started to move.

Chapter Five

LAKE WANNSEE

Hagen stood in the arched doorway of the villa's dining room, considering.

The crystal chandelier overhead was dark. The Oriental carpet underfoot smelled of antiseptic cleaning fluid. Eight Queen Anne chairs stood neatly lined against one wall. Yet even in its current state of disuse, the room gave an impression of muted opulence. It took only a small leap of imagination to picture the space as it had been during the villa's glory days: voices raised in warm conversation, the chime of champagne glasses following a toast. It must have been quite a sight in those days, Hagen thought. He would have liked to see it—to raise his own glass of champagne and, for a fleeting moment, to worry about nothing.

A woman came up behind him, preceded by a waft of perfume. "Gerhard," she said.

He turned. "Angelika."

"Herr Frick is waiting in your office."

He frowned with surprise. "Thank you," he said. "I'll be there in a moment."

The woman departed silently; after a moment her perfume followed. Hagen took another few seconds before leaving the dining room, trying to organize his thoughts. There was too much on his mind these days. Too many secrets, too many half-truths, to keep straight. Had he scheduled an appointment with Herr Frick this morning? He was certain he had not. So why was the man here?

Could it be news about Hobbs, so soon?

There was only one way to find out.

He spent a last moment looking at the quiet dining room, imagining the phantom toasts and the voices raised in cozy camaraderie; then he turned, and moved slowly down the corridor to his office.

"We paid a visit to Wilmersdorf this morning," Frick said. "The man had been there, beyond any doubt. When we came through the door, Frau Gehl was in the process of disposing of bloody bandages. If we'd been an hour faster, we would have him right now."

For some reason, Frick's eyes gave a guilty flicker as he said it.

Hagen noticed this, then dismissed it. He and Frick had been running in very different circles for the past few months. It would be a mistake to think that he could read the man's tacit signals as if nothing had changed. Hagen was more on the wavelength of a bureaucrat, these days, than a soldier. He had sunk that far.

"A radio transmitter was discovered in the attic," Frick continued. "And so it seems fair to assume that Hobbs has been in contact, via the airwaves, with his spymasters in Britain. I am of the opinion that Herr Gehl will be able to enlighten us as to the man's destination—with the proper encouragement. The Gehls are in our custody at Number Eight Prinz Albrecht Strasse. My associate is interrogating them even as we speak."

Hagen nodded approvingly.

"Hobbs has taken their car—a blue Talta. And judging from the bandages, he's been rather seriously wounded. Soon, now, we'll have our man."

"Excellent," Hagen said.

"I thought you would be pleased—and would want to be kept advised of my progress."

Had there been another guilty flicker there? No; it was only in Hagen's mind.

"Thank you, *Herr Kriminal Inspektor.* You've done well."

Frick stood, saluted. "The next time we speak," he said, "I will have even better news."

He left the office, and Hagen looked after him for a few seconds. Then he spun in his chair, to look out through the open window at Lake Wannsee.

Frick had found the man's trail more quickly than he had anticipated. Almost too quickly. Perhaps it had been an error in judgment, to set him on Hobbs' track so soon.

A thin smile flickered across Hagen's face. Error or not, he was pleased that Frick had moved so efficiently. It confirmed his instincts about the man. He had chosen well, in selecting Frick as his protégé.

Others had disappointed him—Katarina Heinrich primary among them. Heinrich had been a remarkable talent, a rare and wonderful discovery. And yet she had turned into the greatest disappointment of Hagen's career. After a year of intensive training at Hamburg, she had been sent to America, almost a decade before, and had promptly disappeared. Had she somehow been discovered, exposed, and arrested? In a way, Hagen would have liked to think so—at least that would not have been a betrayal. But he did not believe that was the case. Instead, he feared, she had simply removed herself from the game. She had been very young, and as a result, very fickle. And perhaps he had made a mistake in becoming too personally involved with the girl. He had confused the issue, in her mind if not in his own.

But Frick would not disappoint him. Initially, the man's insistence on volunteering for duty in Poland had been troubling. It had made Hagen doubt Frick's commitment to the SD. But his reservations had been misplaced. Frick was a good soldier.

And no harm had been done. Hobbs was wounded, on the run in a car that had been identified. Frick was resourceful, and would see the matter to a conclusion. So it would not be long.

He spun around in the chair again, and reached for his silver cigarette case. He lit a cigarette and watched as the wind teased the smoke into ribbons.

He had been working too hard, he thought. The pressure was taking its toll in subtle ways. Dulling his edge.

When this was finished, he would force himself to take a vacation.

FRIEDRICHSTADT, BERLIN

𝔈va consulted the leather-bound address book in her hand, verified that it matched the gilt-edged plaque on the door, and then paused for a moment before knocking.

The block around her was quiet. Gretl, she thought, was probably not even home. Gretl was probably taking advantage of the free day, out somewhere with one of her wealthy boyfriends. If that was the case, then her trip here would have been a waste. She would need to move on and try again later—in which case the chances of being approached and asked for her papers would increase dramatically.

She sincerely hoped that Gretl was home.

She hesitated for another moment, and then knocked twice.

No answer. She shifted her weight from one foot to the other and transferred her case from her right hand to her left. Gretl was not here, and so she would need to stay in Berlin through another night. Her heart sank at the thought; the evening just passed had been trying enough. She had felt the clerk's eyes on her as she had checked into the rooming house—boring into her, filled with questions. A young woman alone checking into a rooming house was suspicious. The best he could have thought was that she was a prostitute. The worst was that she was on the run—the truth.

She had spent the night in the nether region between wakefulness and slumber. In her half-formed dreams, Gestapo agents had come again and again to knock on the door of her room. *Eva*

Bernhardt, they'd said, reading her name off her papers as she stood, sleep-addled, in the doorway. *We have been looking for you, Fräulein. It is a pleasure to make your acquaintance.*

The night had been bad—but the day, if that was possible, had been even worse. She'd been unable to figure out where to go. She had no friends; her family did not know she'd returned to Germany. But her parents' farm in Saxony was the place to which she felt drawn nevertheless. It seemed that there was safety in family. It was a variation on the urge to burrow into bed, she realized, to revert to childhood. In reality, going to the farm would be asking for trouble. If the Abwehr knew what she was, after all, then they would know about her family. She would not be safe there.

For all of the morning and part of the afternoon, she had sat in a park, struggling to hold back her tears, trying to think of an answer. Then, finally, she had decided to try Gretl. It was a desperate decision—but she was in a desperate state.

She turned from the gilt-edged plaque and looked at the street behind her. The street was bare of pedestrians; she felt very exposed standing here. A single car was parked on the Friedrichstadt, a Volkswagen. Except for drawings in newspapers, Eva had never seen one before. It was a curious-looking car, small and compact, with a clean, sleek shape. The Volkswagen—the people's car—had been Adolf Hitler's personal brainchild. "It should look like a beetle," Hitler had commanded. "You have to look to nature to find out what streamlining is." For a brief time, a couple of years before, it had seemed as if every German would soon own one of the affordable little VWs. But then the war had come, and production had been discontinued after only six hundred units. Most of the cars had gone to German generals, prominent businessmen, or Hitler himself.

Prominent businessmen, she thought.

Some of Gretl's boyfriends were prominent businessmen.

And so perhaps Gretl was home after all.

She knocked again, forcefully; this time she kept knocking.

Finally, sounds came from behind the door. A muted giggle, a secretive murmur. Eva stood up straighter. An instant later, the door was opening and Gretl was there, resplendent in a black silk gown with a white orchid on her breast. "Eva!" she said.

"Gretl," Eva said. "I'm sorry to stop by this way . . ."

There was a man behind her, wearing a tuxedo, peering suspiciously over her shoulder. Gretl's eyes flicked to the man, then flicked back to Eva. "It's not the best time," she said. "Can you come back—"

"No. Gretl. No. I can't."

"I'm sorry, Eva, but it's really—"

"I've got nowhere else to go," Eva said, and then added, "Please."

Gretl's brow furrowed. After a moment, she stepped ruefully aside, to allow Eva entrance.

"Joseph, this is Eva. We work together. Eva, this is my friend Joseph." Her voice took on a tone of reprimand. "We were just on our way out," she said.

Joseph was frowning, clearly displeased at the interruption.

"Give us a minute," Gretl said. "Would you mind terribly? Fix yourself a drink."

She took Eva's hand without waiting for an answer, then led her down a long hallway to a spacious bedroom.

The apartment was phenomenal—and far beyond the means of anyone else working at the Rundfunk. Gretl's boyfriends were apparently not lacking in generosity. They passed an antique clock and moved into a bedroom done in white: a pale spread on the bed, cream-colored flowers displayed in a glass vase, and a tremendous wardrobe that looked like, but must not have been, pure ivory. A mahagony dresser, twin nightstands with matching doilies, the vague scent of lilac. Gretl gestured her toward the bed impatiently.

"I hate to be rude," she said. "And it is nice to see you outside of the office, for once. But we were just getting ready to leave. And I'm afraid it's not really the best night for you to come along."

"I'm sorry," Eva said. "I don't mean to interrupt."

"Well—what is it?"

"I need a favor."

"What favor?"

Eva looked down into her lap. What role should she play now? Needy; pitiful, but not too pitiful. She summoned the emotions and then looked up, into Gretl's face.

"Gretl," she said. "I know we hardly know each other . . ."

"My God," Gretl interrupted. "Is that blood?"

"What?"

Gretl leaned down. "Oh. No. It's lipstick."

Eva touched a hand self-consciously to the corner of her mouth.

"You're a mess," Gretl said gravely. "Don't you have a mirror in your flat?"

"Well, I . . ."

"Come here. Look."

She took Eva's hand again and brought her to the framed mirror atop the dresser. Eva saw that her lipstick was horribly smeared, into something approximating the shape of a butterfly.

She felt herself starting to blush. Gretl opened a drawer of the dresser, withdrew a handkerchief, licked it, and began to dab at Eva's cheek.

"You've got to take better care of yourself. How do you expect to find a man looking like that?"

"You're right. I know."

"It's just common sense," Gretl said. "You do the best you can with what you have. Stop fidgeting. Hold still."

"I've got other things on my mind."

"Yes, I can see that. Are you going to tell me, or am I supposed to guess?"

Eva steeled herself. "I need to stay here tonight," she said. "And I need a car."

Gretl lowered the handkerchief, her eyes flickering.

"You know so many men," Eva went on quickly. "I figured that one of them must have a car. And I've got money—"

"This is a joke. Right?"

Their eyes locked in the mirror; Eva slowly shook her head.

Footsteps moved down the hall. "Gretl," a voice said.

"One minute," Gretl said.

"They're going to start without us," Joseph said petulantly.

Gretl went to the door, pushed it closed, and turned back to face Eva.

"A *car?*"

Eva had crossed to the bed. Now she picked up her case and withdrew the five hundred marks she'd received from the man at the River Havel. She tossed it onto the bedspread, and they both looked at the greasy roll of bills.

"Just for a few days," Eva said. "A rental."

Gretl's eyes remained fixed on the money.

"That's five hundred marks," Eva said. "Just get me a car—any car. I'll be out of the way first thing in the morning. You'll never see me again." She licked her lips, then added her first lie: "I'll have a friend bring the car back here. Door-to-door service."

"You quit your job?" Gretl asked, still looking at the money.

"I guess I did. They just don't know it yet."

"What is it, Eva? A family problem?"

"Yes. A family problem."

Gretl finally tore her eyes away from the bills.

"Gretl," the voice called. "I'm going to leave without you, sweetest dumpling, if you don't hurry up."

Gretl turned to the mirror. She adjusted the strap of her gown so that it was falling off her shoulder. Then she pinched at her cheeks, raising the color. She turned back to Eva. "How do I look?"

"Beautiful."

"I'll take care of it," she promised.

"Absolutely not," Joseph said.

He and Gretl were standing in the living room. The wireless had been turned on, playing loud Wagner in an effort to drown out the argument. But his voice climbed over the music, stridently:

"Absolutely not. Forget it."

"Joseph," Gretl said. "She's a friend of mine . . ."

"No."

"Darling, please. It's just for a—"

"I said no."

"Darling," Gretl purred. *"Please . . ."*

Eva stood just outside the doorway, listening.

"As if I don't give you enough," Joseph said.

Across from the living room, in the kitchen, the man's overcoat hung draped across the back of a chair. The last of the day's light shone through venetian blinds, striping it with shadow.

"Do you think it's easy to get champagne these days?" Joseph said. "Do you think this all comes for free? Well, it doesn't. I pay for it—in one way of another. There are other currencies besides money, you know. But of course you do. Look who I'm talking to."

"There's no need to get nasty," Gretl said.

Eva looked at the overcoat. It was hanging slightly askew, weighed down by one pocket. She crossed the hallway and slipped her hand into the coat. Sure enough, the keys were there, cool to the touch.

"It's never enough for you. That's the problem with being an only child, Gretl. You come to think that you deserve everything, and more."

"You know—just forget I asked."

Eva slipped the keys out, turned them over thoughtfully for a moment.

"I will," Joseph said.

"Good. I wish you would."

"Well, then, I will. I'll forget you ever asked."

"Good."

Eva crept toward the front door. A floorboard creaked; her breath caught in her throat. But the Wagner was still playing, the military strains drowning out everything but Joseph's voice:

"But you *did* ask, didn't you? You're always asking, it seems. Always wanting more. Sometimes I wonder, Gretl. Sometimes I wonder just what *I* get from our arrangement."

Eva stepped outside, the keys clutched tightly in one hand. She jogged to the Volkswagen without looking back over her shoulder. Even from the street, she could hear the man's voice, still rising:

"If I've got a limit, then you're going to find it, aren't you? Never happy with what I offer. Never happy with what you've got."

The keys fit.

She got into the car, almost bumping her head on the low roof. The VW was tiny. She tossed her case on the passenger-side seat, then started the engine.

"Why don't you ask one of your other boyfriends? You've got plenty. Oh, you may not think I know. But I know. I know more than you think, my sweetest dumpling. Maybe one of them is an easier touch than old Joseph. Maybe one of them has got a car for you. Or for your *friend*. If it *is* for your friend. You've got lots of friends, don't you? You make friends so easily . . ."

Eva smiled despite herself. She immediately brushed it from her face. There was nothing amusing about what she was doing to Gretl. But she was desperate. She had no other choice.

She had left the money on the bed, at least.

"I think I've changed my mind about tonight," Joseph was saying. "I think I'd rather go alone, than with a girl who's ready to take advantage of me every chance she gets."

Eva hadn't driven a car for years, not since she had used her father's truck around the farm. But it was like riding a bicycle, wasn't it? Once you learned, you never forgot.

She switched on the headlamps by mistake, switched them off, then tried to pull away from the curb. The Volkswagen coughed and stalled. She reached for the keys again, twisting them. The engine rolled, caught. She aimed it into the street and drifted forward.

Gretl, she thought. *I'm sorry.*

But the smile winked back, for just a fraction of a second, before she banished it from her face for good.

WILMERSDORF

itler's Reichsautobahn was the world's first superhighway system, and a marvel of engineering; it had been built by members of the Labor Service without the benefit of machinery. But what the system offered in ease of travel, to Hobbs' present way of thinking, was compromised by a lack of privacy.

He left the autobahn not far outside Berlin, in favor of serpentine back roads that made the Talta jounce and rattle like a set of castanets. For nearly an hour, he was able to convince himself that he would be secure enough on these roads. During that time he passed no motorized traffic, a single bicycle, and an old woman pulling a small cart.

Then, all at once, he couldn't convince himself any longer. The Talta, of course, was an invitation to trouble. As he had been pulling away from the Gehls' house in Wilmersdorf, he had seen a black Mercedes drawing up behind him. For a panicky moment, he had believed that his time had run out—for the car belonged to the Gestapo. And the Talta, with its rear windshield missing, with the blood of the SS staining the bent fender, was as good as a beacon advertising his presence.

But the Mercedes had not followed him. Instead it had moved to the curb; two men in black suits had come out. The last thing he had seen was the men striding purposefully up the walk to the Gehls' house. So it wasn't his time that had run out, not yet. For the Gehls, however . . .

He didn't want to think about it.

He needed to get rid of the car. Stay focused on the moment.

But the thought of abandoning the Talta, with his leg in its current condition, was not an alluring one. Gehl had helped to remove the bullet, wash the wound, and apply bandages; but neither of them were doctors. Even the slow steady pressure of keeping his foot on the gas made his thigh throb angrily.

Bollixed it all up, he thought.

He had to get rid of the car. Choose one of these leafy glens, hide the Talta in the foliage, and then . . .

. . . and then what?

Walk? Not on this leg; not for long.

Catch a ride? There wasn't a cover story in the world that would explain a wounded man, speaking schoolboy German, walking alone along the side of these back-country roads.

So he kept driving.

The day cooled as clouds passed in front of the sun. The breeze coming through the empty rear windshield took on an icy tinge. Presently he felt the first stirrings of an appetite. He reached for the satchel on the passenger-side seat, dug through it, and removed a hunk of bread. He ate half of it and then tucked it back into the bag. His supplies were limited; he would need to make them last.

He didn't even have a gun. He had thrown it away when it had run out of ammunition. Stupid.

He shrugged off his doubts as best as he could, and kept driving.

As the sky darkened by degrees, the doubts returned. Had Eva gotten away quickly enough? Or had he doomed her, with his sloppy contact? Nothing to be gained, of course, by thinking about it. Either she had or she hadn't.

But he couldn't help himself.

He had doomed her, of course. He had caused one hell of a scene outside her apartment. She would have needed to move like the wind to avoid arrest, after a scene like that. She had already been under observation, after all. Why observation, and not arrest? That part he couldn't figure out. Perhaps Canaris had wanted to use her as bait . . . as flypaper, to attract spies like Hobbs himself.

And he had also doomed the Gehls. The SS would find the radio transmitter in the attic; they would have their proof. Even at this moment, no doubt, Ernst Gehl was in the basement of Number 8 Prinz Albrecht Strasse, suffering the thumbscrews and fingernail splints of the Gestapo. Would the man tell them the location of the extraction site? If he did, then there was hardly a point in continuing. But perhaps Gehl would not tell. And what other choice was there? Giving up. Which was really no choice at all.

His depression deepened.

It was not too late. He was still free. He had passed the message to Eva. Now he could only hope that she would be able to shake her surveillance and reach Gothmund, and that he would be there to meet her.

As the sun sank lower in the sky, the choice of what to do with the Talta was taken away from him: The car ran out of petrol.

When he realized what was happening, Hobbs immediately coaxed the car off the road. He pointed it at a stand of linden and oak, twenty feet distant, and then watched apprehensively as it rolled forward. Yet another brilliant maneuver, he thought. He had become so caught up in his own thoughts that he'd neglected to pay attention to the most obvious factor of all: an empty gas tank.

Mercifully, the Talta rolled all the way into the stand of trees before failing. He pressed the brake and then sat, listening to the tick of the cooling engine.

It was time, he supposed, to take a walk.

But he didn't move. He stayed behind the wheel, looking out at the trees surrounding him. It was a better hiding place than he might have expected. From the road he would be all but invisible. Perhaps he would do better to spend the night here. They would be looking for him, once they realized that the Gehls' car was missing. But they would never suspect that he had simply pulled off the road so close to Berlin. Perhaps the search would pass him by.

Simplicity is effective.

In the morning he would cut a walking stick from one of the saplings, then head back to the road and try to catch a ride. And if anyone was trusting enough to give him one, that would be their misfortune. There was no cover story in the world, after all, that could explain him. So he would need to kill the driver—with his bare hands, he supposed—and take the car.

If anyone was trusting enough to pull over.

The air was growing cold. The lack of a rear windshield left the interior of the car open to the weather. But he would survive.

In the morning, he thought. He would figure something out in the morning.

He ate the rest of his bread, drank some of the water, then lit a cigarette and leaned back in the seat, trying to get comfortable—and failing.

He had doomed her, with his sloppy contact. And she had been an innocent.

He finished the cigarette and closed his eyes. Sleep came in choppy waves. With the sleep, his defenses went down; and with the defenses down came the guilty memories.

Some time later, he sat up with a jolt.

Still in the Talta; still night. He had pulled himself out of sleep, he realized, with an act of will. He had been back in his East End garret, suggesting to Eva that she come onto Oldfield's payroll. It seemed that his mind was determined to make him relive the moment over and over again.

He squirmed in the seat. One leg was asleep—the wounded leg. When he changed position, it began to tingle with pins and needles. At least he could still feel it.

He found himself looking at his own reflection in the windshield. He looked pale, unshaven, and haggard. This would be the death of him, he thought suddenly. He would never make it back to England alive.

What in the name of God was he doing here?

He had come for Eva, of course. Because he had finally grown up. A man could drift from cause to cause, and from woman to woman, for only so long. Eventually he reached a point when he was ready for more. And more, as he understood it, meant settling down. A wife. A family.

There were other reasons as well, he supposed. His nights spent with the BUF had convinced him that Fascism was a fool's cause, a crutch for the weak-minded—and a dangerous one, for there were many in the world even more weak-minded than Hobbs himself. But he could not quite convince himself that King and Country were his primary motivations in coming to Germany. Those who risked their lives for any ideology—be it Fascism, Bolshevism, or the glory of the Crown—were fooling themselves if they thought that they were acting for reasons other than personal.

So it was for Eva. This was not the first time Hobbs had found himself spending a night alone, without a proper roof; but he was determined that it would be one of the last.

Had he known when he had first seen her that she would be any different from the others? The idea was tempting—love at first sight, a comforting thought—but unfortunately it hadn't been the case. It had been just a straight recruitment to Hobbs, one in a string of similar recruitments. He had been paying a visit to his old mates in Guildford in an effort to keep up local connections; his value to Oldfield had been dependent on keeping up such old ties, on maintaining the trust of his various ne'er-do-well acquaintances. He had been sitting in the Royal Oak pub with Roland Lewis and Art Moore when he had seen the pretty redheaded girl go walking by the window—according to the barmaid, a governess for the Carmody children, who had been in England at that point for only two weeks.

He had approached her on some slim pretext that he couldn't even recall. As the months had passed, and they had evolved from acquaintances to friends to lovers, her possible value had become increasingly clear—Eva was a German, after all, and a smart one, with a passion for integrity. When her position in Guildford had ended, she had decided to stay on in London, at Hobbs' urging, for another year. Finally had come the recruitment itself, that night in his flat in the East End. But even then he hadn't realized how much he had come to care for her. It was only after she had gone . . .

He winced. His goddamned leg. Now the pins and needles were passing, and it was beginning to throb again.

He settled back into the seat. Dawn was still a long way away. But he couldn't stand the thought of returning to the dream, returning to the memory.

He kept his eyes open long after they'd begun to ache, staring at the whispering leaves around the car.

Chapter Six

THE FINCH PUB, WHITEHALL

Arthur Deacon sat alone in a booth, staring into his pint of Guinness. An ashtray near his hand contained the butts of six cigarettes. A seventh burned between his fingers, forgotten.

He remembered the cigarette only when the ember scorched his knuckles. Then he swore, ground it out among the remains of the others, tossed his dark hair back from his forehead, and knuckled briefly at his brown eyes. He checked his watch. Only five minutes remained before his appointment with Oldfield, and he still had not made up his mind.

He lit another cigarette, tossed back his hair again—Mary was always nagging him to get it cut, but somehow he could never find the time—then returned to staring into his pint.

His reverie was broken when Margery Lewis slid into the booth across from him. Margery looked a few pounds heavier than the last time Deacon had seen her, as if the rationing had skipped her altogether. But her lipstick was as bright and tarty as ever, her face as wide and round and homely. He wondered, in that first moment, what he had ever seen in her. Then she leaned forward so he could light her cigarette; her dress scooped down in front to reveal her ample bosom, and he remembered.

"Arthur," she said. "Look at you, so deep in thought."

He nodded. "Margery," he said.

"Sitting here frowning like a funeral director." She dragged on her cigarette, exhaled around a dry smile. "I dare say marriage doesn't agree with you."

"Bugger off," he said pleasantly.

"I'd be glad to, love. But I might need a hand. Is that an offer?"

"You said it yourself, Margery—I'm married now."

"Happily?"

"Very much so. Thank you."

"Then why the long face?"

He shrugged, sipped his pint, and tapped an ash into the ashtray.

"I hear you've got a son," she said. "I suppose I should say congratulations."

"Thank you."

"*Should* say. Not *will* say."

"Gracious as ever. Dear heart."

"Let's slip out back, into the alley. For old time's sake."

"Margery, love—I've got to go. Take care."

He stood. She looked after him as he shrugged into his coat, tipped an imaginary hat, and went.

Once outside Deacon cupped his hand over his nose and blew into it. The beer was still on his breath. Oldfield would not approve. He dug through his pockets, found a sprig of spearmint, and popped it into his mouth.

Before taking the short stroll to Leconfield House, he stood for a moment, chewing on the spearmint and thinking. He had told Oldfield he would have his decision by today. Yet Deacon felt no closer to making the decision than he had a week before, when Oldfield had first approached him about the mission.

He found himself looking at his hands. They were open, turned up to face the muttering sky. A fine metaphor for his predicament, he thought—six in the one hand, half a dozen in the other.

On the first hand were responsibility, common sense, and prudence. He had never met William Hobbs in person, but the man's reputation had preceded him. If Hobbs was half the lout that most of the men around Whitehall believed him to be, then undertaking the mission would be tantamount to committing suicide. For Hobbs, according to the conventional wisdom around MI6, was working for the Nazis. He had been dodgy even before he had gone over there; and since his arrival, much to Oldfield's chagrin, he had fallen off schedule. Even if he *was* still loyal, he lacked something in steadiness. By trying to take such a man out of Germany, Deacon might well be handing the Nazis a prototype aircraft, not to mention an experienced RAF pilot. His wife and son would be left without a father.

That was on the one hand.

But Deacon had never been renowned for his prudence. And on the other hand were the nobler virtues: justice, courage, loyalty, and honor. Assuming that Hobbs was not working for the Nazis—that he had a lion's heart beating somewhere under his con man's façade, and that he had successfully completed his own operation in Germany—then he would need to be evacuated. As would the Bernhardt girl, who might possibly be in possession of intelligence that could help them to win the war.

On the one hand: responsibility, common sense, and prudence. On the other: justice, courage, loyalty, and honor.

It was really no contest at all.

He spat out the spearmint and went to keep his meeting.

The old-fashioned lift carried him to the fifth floor with its ancient gears creaking loudly; Deacon operated the lever himself.

He had not set foot inside Leconfield House for several months, since before the start of the war—but little around the War Office, he thought, seemed to have changed. The teak-inlaid halls still smelled musty and close. The men and women sitting behind their heavy black typewriters still looked weary and distracted. The crossword puzzle of that morning's *Times* was in evidence, in various stages of completion, on the corner of nearly every desk.

He marched down the corridor and then paused before a door at the end: the Director General's office. He knocked twice, waited for the light above the door to flash green, and then stepped into an airy chamber dominated by a long polished conference table, with heavy red sashes framing a tall, rain-streaked window.

Cecil Oldfield was bent over a map on the conference table. He beckoned Deacon closer without looking up.

"Three hundred feet exactly," Oldfield said, pointing to a spot on the map. "I'm afraid it doesn't leave much room for error."

Deacon joined him as the door closed softly behind them.

The map represented the town of Gothmund, huddled against the Trave River on the outskirts of Lübeck. The three hundred feet to which Oldfield had referred represented the field in which Deacon would be landing his prototype Lysander—or trying to land it, as the case may be.

"As far as we know, the field's empty," Oldfield said. "Too marshy for farming. But of course, we haven't had any trustworthy firsthand reports for too long now."

Deacon leaned down, looking closer. "Marshy," he repeated.

"Don't worry; the thaw hasn't taken yet. You shouldn't get stuck in any mud. We hope."

"Hm."

"So. Have you reached a decision?"

Deacon's mouth felt suddenly dry. When he spoke, however, his voice was clear. "I'm game," he said.

"Good," Oldfield said smoothly. He hardly sounded surprised. "If all goes well, you'll be on the ground for less than a minute. The girl should be waiting there with Hobbs. There may be others with them: perhaps the fisherman, Brandt, perhaps even the OKW clerk." He looked up, into Deacon's eyes from a distance of about six inches. Oldfield was a gallows-thin man with muttonchop sideburns and a ruddy complexion. From this close distance, he smelled vigorously of tobacco. "Or perhaps a division or two of Hitler's finest," he said sourly.

Deacon nodded briefly.

"Now here"—Oldfield's finger moved over the map—"is Brandt's home, along a road called the Fischerweg, which runs in front of a row of little cottages. If things go wrong—terribly wrong—you might want to make a try for it. It's less than a quarter mile from the landing zone. I'll give you some information concerning the remnants of our underground network in Germany, such as it is. If worse comes to worst, you'll take the girl into hiding. Then try to get over the border with her, wherever you can manage it. Although if it comes to that . . ."

Deacon nodded again. He straightened, suddenly feeling considerably older than his twenty-six years. "When do I go?" he asked.

"Three days. Try to get some rest before then, hm? You'll want your eyes as sharp as possible for this one."

"I'll do my best."

"Remember," Oldfield said. "No repercussions if you come back empty-handed."

Deacon smiled to himself. These strange times, he thought, had even taken a toll on an old bulldog such as Oldfield.

"Uncle Cecil," he said. "I do believe you're getting soft, in your old age."

On the way back to Bayswater, Deacon found his mind roaming.

He thought for a time of his wife and his newborn son. Thinking of them was a luxury; he allowed himself exactly three minutes. Then he harrumphed, rearranging himself in the backseat of the Bentley, and forced his mind in a new direction. If he thought of his family for too long, he might find an excuse to change his mind about accepting the mission. And that would not do.

He looked at the balding crown on the back of his driver's head, thinking for a few empty seconds of nothing in particular; then his mind turned to the upcoming operation.

If it had been a suicide mission, he would not have accepted it. He had responsibilities now, as his wife was so keen on pointing out. But it was not a suicide mission. Just damned close.

He remembered his first meeting with Oldfield on the subject, a week before. His uncle had given it to him straight, as they had stood inside the swaying army surplus tent and inspected the prototype Lysander Mark III.

"Lately," Oldfield said, "I've been thinking I was wrong in the head to work with Hobbs in the first place. But while I had him in my sight, I felt right enough about him. He has a way of putting people at ease. A skill he learned on the street, no doubt. Now that he's gone, however, I've been wondering. He might be rotten to the core; and even if he's not, he may prove incapable of doing what we need done."

Deacon had been looking over the plane as Oldfield had spoken. The Lysander had been modified with an external fuel tank holding 150 gallons, providing an endurance of eight hours' flying time. A ladder had been fitted to the fuselage to allow quick access to and from the ground. All in all, the prototype had turned out brilliantly. Oldfield had mentioned that they would be doing up more of the little planes in this fashion, in case the war dragged on.

"This is an important one," Oldfield continued. "Our intelligence on the Wehrmacht's plans is sketchy at best. I've got a memo from Deuxième Bureau on my desk predicting a mid-March offensive against the Netherlands and Belgium, to be accompanied by air attacks on London and Paris. Then another correcting the information: no offensive against Belgium, but a certain attack on the Netherlands. Then another warning of an attack at the Maginot Line, with no movement in Belgium *or* the Netherlands. The truth is, it's a big bloody mess."

They'd strolled leisurely back across Heathrow airfield following the brief inspection. Heathrow had been the perfect site for their meeting: modest to the point of humility, featuring no permanent buildings, let alone a runway. Nearby Heston and Hanworth Park were the places that came to mind when one thought of an airfield. And so those were the places that the Fifth Columnists might be watching. Heathrow itself was below suspicion.

Before leaving Oldfield, that day, Deacon had paused to look back at the single army tent that concealed the prototype Lysander. A drizzle had started, tossing the tails of his Burberry coat.

"Think it through," Oldfield said. "Talk it over with the wife. See what you decide."

In retrospect, Deacon realized that Oldfield had known him better than he had known himself. He had been counting on Deacon's pride. Pilots did not turn away from dangerous missions; they lived for them.

Deacon suffered no shortage of pride. Not only was he the best pilot he knew in the RAF, but he was one of the few, in this Phony War, with any combat experience. He had been a part of the confetti campaign, dropping propaganda leaflets onto Germany. Not that everybody would have considered that *combat experience*, of course. A joke had been making the rounds lately, summing up the peculiar lot of the confetti campaign pilots. An airman, the joke went, found himself in serious trouble after dropping a bundle of leaflets without separating them first. The brick of pamphlets had plummeted straight down onto Berlin like a paper bomb. *Good God*, the airman's superior said in chastising him: *You might have killed someone!*

Deacon smiled, very slightly, in the back of the Bentley.

It was important to keep one's sense of humor, in strange times such as these.

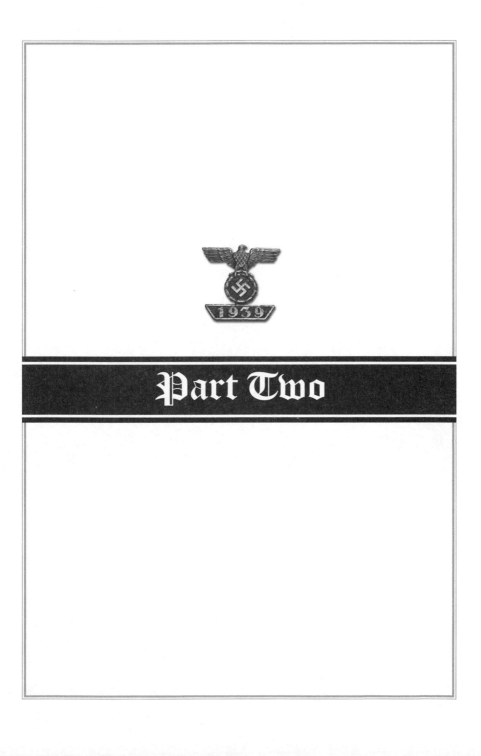

Part Two

Chapter Seven

PRINZ ALBRECHT STRASSE

Herr Inspektor?" a voice said.

The voice belonged to Hauptmann, standing in the doorway with his russet hair slightly disheveled, a small spot of blood staining the lapel of his otherwise spotless uniform.

"Herr Hauptmann," Frick said. "The interrogation is finished?"

"Frau Gehl has left this world, *Herr Inspektor.* But her husband is still with us."

"And?"

"He has admitted to sheltering the Engländer, and to providing him with supplies. And he has confirmed that Hobbs moved on very shortly before our arrival yesterday. He has only the car, some food, and some water. According to Herr Gehl, the man is unarmed."

"His destination?"

A wrinkle of frustration creased Hauptmann's forehead. "Gehl claims ignorance. When I mention the radio transmitter, he denies ever having seen it."

"But it was found in his home."

"The man is stubborn, *Herr Inspektor.* Surprisingly so."

"Is he aware of the fate of his wife?"

"He is. And since her death, he has become even more obstinate. Perhaps it was a miscalculation on my part . . ."

"Do not concern yourself," Frick said. "I will pay a visit to the man myself as soon as I've finished here."

"Thank you, *Herr Inspektor.*"

When Hauptmann had gone, Frick turned his attention back to the file on his desk. It was a description of Salon Kitty, the premier brothel in Berlin. Salon Kitty was a favorite haunt of top-ranking Gestapo agents and visiting diplomats. But according to the file, the brothel might also serve a more nefarious purpose. The author of the report put forth the theory that in reality Salon Kitty was a pet project of Reinhard Heydrich's, and a front for the SD. If one were to look behind the walls, the report posited, one might possibly find a network of hidden microphones and tape recorders. Heydrich might be bolstering his secret security files on the Gestapo by collecting ammunition for blackmail.

It was, Frick knew, completely true. And this was one reason that Hagen had placed him in the Gestapo, so that he could intercept material like this file before it garnered too much attention. He reached for a pen and scratched a note in the margin of the report: *Speculative.* After thinking for a few seconds, he added a postscript. *This type of report fosters suspicion between the security organs of the Reich. In all future . . .*

He finished writing his note in the margin, and then pushed back and went to pay a visit to Herr Gehl.

The infamous "house prison" of Number 8 Prinz Albrecht Strasse consisted of thirty-nine cells in the building's cellar: damp concrete chambers smelling of niter, frightened sweat, and human excrement. Frick came off the staircase, paused for a moment to let his eyes adjust to the crepuscular gloom, conferred briefly with a guard, and was escorted to the cell containing Ernst Gehl.

Gehl was strapped to a steel table, held fast by leather restraints. Beside the table was a single chair. Beside the chair was a medical tray lined with implements. In the cell's corner, obscured by shadows, stood a piece of equipment—rubber-clad cables, an electrical transformer, metal clips smeared with clotting blood.

Frick nodded at the guard, put a hand on the chair, pulled it to the edge of the steel table, and sat.

Gehl's eyes were closed. His face was bruised; one cheek was torn open. Through the gaping skin, Frick could see two of the man's teeth, yellowly luminous in the faint light coming from the corridor.

"Herr Gehl," he said softly. "Are you awake?"

Gehl's eyes opened. They turned, slowly, to Frick.

"I understand that you are being difficult," Frick said. "I have come to help you understand that there is nothing to be gained by it."

Gehl looked at him for a moment, coolly, and then closed his eyes again.

Frick drew back, considering. He rubbed at his chin, and then leaned forward again.

"A radio transmitter was discovered in your house," he said. "One assumes that you used it to contact your allies in England. Is this correct?"

No response.

"I hardly need your confirmation," Frick said gently, "on so obvious a matter. But I do require something else from you. I would like to know the destination of the Engländer. Since the radio was in your possession, I believe that you must be aware of this."

Somebody in an adjoining cell was crying quietly. Frick blocked it out. He scooted the chair a bit closer to Gehl. Something was dotting the man's chest—small off-whitish clumps that he thought at first might be more teeth. Then he realized that they were fragments of rock salt, which the man had spat out when the current had passed through his body.

"Was it Teiresias who said it?" Frick asked. "'When wisdom brings no profit, to be wise is to suffer.' Your wife, I believe, has already learned this lesson. You are aware of her fate. Hm?"

Again, no reaction. Gehl looked almost peaceful. Frick felt his temper starting to rise. He breathed in and out, calming himself.

And then he saw that Gehl was smiling.

A vein pulsed in Frick's temple. "Does that amuse you?" he asked.

No reaction; but the smile stayed.

The vein pulsed again. A minute passed, and then another. The smile left Gehl's face in degrees, like autumn leaves picked up in clutches by a cold wind.

When Frick spoke again, his voice was silky, and ripe with sympathy.

"I believe it was a mistake to let your wife suffer. Had she not been involved, you already would have cooperated with us. But now you have a personal reason for being stubborn. Is this a fair assessment?"

Gehl's eyes fluttered open. His lips parted; he whispered something. Frick leaned forward, trying to catch it.

When Gehl spat, the bloody saliva took Frick full in his right eye.

He pushed back again, swiping at his face. For a moment, he held perfectly still. Then he began to quiver with rage.

The smile was playing around Gehl's lips again.

Frick reached and covered Gehl's nose and mouth with one broad hand.

The man did not understand his place. He did not understand what he was dealing with, here. But Frick would make him understand.

After a few seconds, Gehl began to produce noises. Frick held his palm tight against the man's face, muffling them. The hands tugged against the leather restraints. Then the feet started to move, the heels drumming a ragged tattoo against the metal.

Frick pressed harder. He would make his point. His time, unlike Hauptmann's, was valuable. He did not have twenty-four hours to waste in getting his answers.

Now Gehl's face, beneath his hand, was turning red. He was

beginning to understand, Frick thought. Frick was not Hauptmann; he was not a child. And this was not a game.

Then Gehl tried a new tactic—he went limp. The florid color in his cheeks turned suddenly blotchy, as if blood vessels had broken. A fine trick, Frick thought. Some sort of physiological reaction, manufactured by necessity. But he would not be fooled. He left his hand over the man's nose and mouth and counted, very deliberately, to twenty. Then he took his hand away.

"Now," he said. "I will ask one last time."

Gehl continued with his act. His hands in the leather restraints stayed limp. He was holding his breath; his chest did not move.

Frick bent closer, until his face was only inches from Gehl's. A remarkable act, he thought. Gehl's eyelids were half-shuttered, showing glassy pupils beneath. He still had not taken a breath. Amazing, the lengths to which a man would go to make pain stop.

It took another few moments for Frick to realize that Gehl was not acting—Gehl was dead.

When he realized it, something close to panic took him. He backed away quickly, the chair whining against the concrete floor. He had gone too far; he had taken the man's life. It was not his fault, of course. Gehl was old and weak, and Hauptmann had already been at him for a day. And yet it was a mistake—for with Gehl dead, they would have no way of discovering Hobbs' destination.

Your second mistake, his mind offered helpfully. *You forgot about the file. You could have stopped the Britisher earlier if only—*

But that was not a memory. That was a dream. He had not known the Engländer's location until the very morning he had gone to apprehend him; and by then it already had been too late.

He did not make mistakes. These were tricks. Somebody, somehow, was tricking him.

He stood up. The problem was not insoluble. He would find Hobbs some other way—and then this small miscalculation, made by somebody else, would be of no consequence.

On his way out the guard caught his attention. "*Herr Kriminal Inspektor*," he said. "You are finished with the prisoner?"

"Yes," Frick said. "I am finished."

"Are we to keep him here?"

"He's dead. Get rid of him."

He climbed the stairs without looking back to see the man's reaction.

Behind his desk, he frowned with consternation. That smell again . . . the sweet/sour odor of fresh bread . . . and something behind his eyes, pulsing.

The phone on his desk chimed softly.

He answered. "Frick," he said, and listened.

After hanging up, he thought for a moment, then opened the drawer of his desk and withdrew a well-oiled Luger.

The Talta had been discovered, abandoned not far outside Berlin. If the Engländer was on foot, it would be an easy matter to track him with dogs. If he had found another vehicle, then the matter would be slightly more complex—but only slightly. The Gestapo's network of *Vertrauensmänner* ran through every level of German society, from the lowliest cobbler to the highest-born aristocrat. Something as considerable as a disappearing car would not avoid being reported for long. And when the report came in, through whatever channel, it would be brought to Frick's attention.

And as for the other . . . strangeness . . .

His tongue came out and ran over his lips.

Later. When he had the time for it.

He left the office, and went to find Hauptmann, and some dogs.

WISMAR, MECKLENBURG

Hobbs woke up.

At first he didn't know where he was. The car was still moving; but it was drawing to a stop. He sat straight, blinking the sleep from his eyes, and then looked over at the driver.

She was smiling back at him. "Home, sweet home," she said in English.

Outside, the sky was dark. They were at a house, he realized, on a hill overlooking a town. He yawned, reached for his satchel, then threw open his door.

The hill sloped down to a scatter of thatched roofs, a cobbled main street, a town square surrounded by buildings with brick façades. A massive red church was illuminated by the moonlight, with a tremendous sculpture out front depicting a man and a dragon. Farther off, beyond the town, the land continued to roll. Windmills dotted the landscape, cutting the night air with a soft, soothing motion.

The woman had come around to his side of the car. She was a statuesque brunette, a few years older than Hobbs, with a vaguely horselike face. Her smile, full of prominent white teeth, was meaningful and sly. There was a secret between them, that smile said.

"Come on," she said, and led him to the door.

The woman's name was Paula Kahr.

They had talked for almost an hour, that afternoon, before he had fallen asleep. That was why her smile was so loaded with meaning, of course. He had brought out his entire repertoire of faltering German in an effort to convince her that he was a local. She had corrected him good-naturedly: *Guten Tag* when he had said *Guten Abend, Wieviel Uhr ist es?* when he had said *Wieviel kostet das?* Finally, she had taken the lead and taught him a few things. *Ich spreche nicht sehr gut Deutsch.* She had made him repeat it several times, and then translated: *I don't speak German very well.*

Then the first of the slow, meaningful smiles.

They moved into the house; Paula reached for a lamp. Hobbs found his eyes drawn immediately to a fireplace with a granite hearth, with an old rifle hanging above the mantel. Beside the fireplace was a pyrographic table featuring two wine-bottle candlesticks, a low sofa with a quilt, and a faded carpet on a wooden floor.

"Sit down," she said. "Make yourself comfortable." Then she moved into the next room with a casual flip of her hair.

Instead of sitting, Hobbs went to the rifle hanging above the fireplace. It was an old M1917 Enfield, well preserved. *All the way from England*, he thought. Looking at it gave him a pleasurable tingle of nostalgia.

He took it down and turned it over in his hands. The Enfield was the same model he had used as a boy. No great surprise to find it here; the M1917 was one of the finest firearms in the world. Hunters across the globe collected them, treasuring them.

The gun was loaded with a standard five-round internal

magazine. His eyes flicked to a small lockbox resting on the hearth. He surreptitiously tried the lid. There were more magazines inside the lockbox. He closed it and hung the rifle on the wall again.

From the next room came the sounds of a knife on a cutting board; then a cork being worked from a bottle. A faint sound, but to Hobbs' ears a recognizable one. He grinned and went to sit on the low sofa.

After a moment, the reality of his situation impressed itself on him, and the grin slipped away.

He had lost his nerve again. He should have strangled the woman and taken her car. But what had Paula done to deserve that? She had stopped to help a stranger on the side of the road. She was innocent.

He tried to recall the story he had told to explain himself. At first it had been something about his car breaking down. He had identified himself as a piano tuner, he remembered. But even then he had known that she wasn't buying it. He had tried to elaborate, but had succeeded only in digging himself deeper. He was a piano tuner for the Prussian State Theater. But he had spent some time in England, which explained his lack of German. In fact, he was originally from England. But he had been in Germany for twelve years already. He had never been good with languages . . .

Paula hadn't seemed to care that he was lying to her.

She had told him that her husband had gone off to join the war. She had suggested that he might want to work on his German a bit, so that he'd have a better chance of convincing the next stranger he met that he was a local. She had told him that he looked underfed. What he needed, she ventured, was a good meal.

Then he'd fallen asleep—inconceivable but true; the night spent in the Talta had been far from restful—and now here they were. But what did she think he was? A deserter? That would explain her lack of interest in the truth—but not his lack of facility with the language.

A spy?

If she thought he was a spy and she'd brought him home anyway, then she was mad.

Perhaps she was mad.

She came back into the room, balancing a bottle of wine, a plate of sliced bratwurst, and two glasses.

"I hope it's not too sweet," she said, filling the glasses. "The best varieties have an almond flavor. But this isn't one of the best."

As he ate, she watched, holding her glass and talking.

"If you want my opinion," she said—her English very good; her English almost flawless—"there's nothing wrong with older women and younger men. As long as it's within a few years, I mean. As a matter of fact, my husband is younger than I. By three months. So really, we're about the same age. But if you want to get technical, he's the baby. How old are you?"

Hobbs looked up, swallowing the food in his mouth. "Thirty-five," he said.

"Well; so I'm thirty-six. Within a few years, it's no problem. If Barbara Stanwyck can do it, so can I."

Hobbs turned his attention back to his plate. "Where did you say your husband is?"

"Off goose-stepping with the rest of the boys. Listen: *Paradeschritt.* Try it."

"*Paradeschritt*," he said.

117

"Good. That means goose-stepping. Try this one. *Liebhaber.*"

"*Liebhaber*," he said.

"That means lover," she said, and gave another crafty, loaded smile.

Then back to the inconsequence of age difference. Why, Thomas Wolfe had taken a woman nineteen years his senior, the greatest love of his life . . .

Hobbs found his pack of cigarettes. Only three remained. The brand was British. But Paula already knew more than she was saying. He lit one without making any special effort to hide the pack, and smoked it to the nub.

Soon after, they moved to the bedroom.

The woman was forward—too forward, for his tastes—but it had been so long that he managed to overlook it. She peeled off his clothes, plastering kisses on his neck. If he smelled overripe, it didn't seem to bother her. When she took off his pants, he remembered the bandage on his thigh. But that also did not deter her. Her fingers brushed past it and then she was pulling the trousers over his shoes, tearing them off.

There was no light in the bedroom. That made it easier.

At some point, he found himself looking at her teeth. She was astride him and her face was contorted, as if she was in terrible pain. Her lips were skinned back like an animal's. *Horse teeth,* he thought. He quickly tried to think of something else—anything else. But after that, all he could see was the teeth.

When he started to go soft, she stopped moving. "What's wrong?" she said.

He shook his head. Those teeth were still in his mind. And below them, somewhere, the thought of Eva.

He rolled over on top of her, determined to regain his

momentum. But it was too late. He had finished without finishing. And the woman knew it. Over the next few minutes, she became increasingly motionless. He closed his eyes, trying to conjure a fantasy. But it was Eva's face that kept returning. Eva—goddamn her all to hell.

Finally, he gave up and rolled away, panting. They lay still, staring into the darkness.

"Well," Paula said.

Hobbs turned over, away from her, and closed his eyes.

Presently, he was aware of her getting out of bed and moving into the other room. A moment after that, the sound of a door opening, furtively. It closed with a quiet click.

He sat up, suddenly wide awake.

On her way out, Paula took her car keys.

She had the quilt from the sofa wrapped around her shoulders. She stood for an instant, her teeth chattering in the night, and then ran for the neighbor's house.

Lights were still on inside. Emmy Hetzler answered her knock. Emmy, the local seamstress, took one look at Paula, blinked stupidly, and then took another, slower look.

Behind her, Hermann Hetzler, Emmy's husband, was talking.

"Friedburg, the old fool, says it can't be done. But he's just lazy. Two good strong horses and a rope, and we'll bring the place right to the ground."

The old Scheppel place, Paula thought. Over the past month alone, two children from town had been hurt playing around the old ruins. Fire had taken the place almost three years before; the Scheppels had deserted it. Any day now, the whole thing would come crashing down, and whatever children were playing inside when that happened would be worse than hurt.

In recent weeks, the townsfolk had been debating the matter of what to do about the ruins with ever-increasing exigency. Some felt that the Scheppels, who had since relocated in Hamburg, should come back and solve the problem themselves. Others, like the tailor Friedburg, felt that the Gestapo, once notified, would be glad to remove the debris. But Hermann Hetzler and his contingent felt that it was a town problem, and that town problems should remain town problems.

"Tomorrow I'm going to get some boys together and go have another look. Two horses, I'm telling you; that's all it's going to take. Then Friedburg can eat his words. The lazy old fool."

"My God," Emmy said. "What happened to you?"

Paula moved into the house, shivering.

"Town business belongs to the town," Hermann said decisively. "Once you let those Hitler-Heilers get their foot in the door, they never let you forget. Mark my words. They come back the next week and expect—"

"Hermann. Look at this."

The man looked up from his table, saw Paula with the quilt wrapped around her shoulders, and came out of his seat.

"What happened?" Emmy asked again, leading Paula to the couch.

"A man," Paula said. "He's in my house."

"What man?"

"An Engländer. He . . . he took liberties with me."

"*Gott im Himmel*," Emmy breathed. "You poor dear."

"An Engländer?" Hermann said. "Where is he now?"

"Still there."

Hermann turned and stalked deeper into the cottage. Emmy stroked Paula's hair, brushing it off her forehead.

"You poor dear. Are you all right? Has he hurt you?"

"No . . . just my pride. I'm all right."

"You poor dear. Come on, lie down. Cover yourself. We'll take care of it."

Hermann appeared again, a rifle in his hands. His eyes locked with his wife's.

"Hermann," Emmy said. "Don't get any ideas. Call the *Regierungsrat.*"

Hermann shook his head, checking the gun's load. "Town business," he said, "is town business."

"Hermann—"

But he was already gone.

Emmy looked after him for a few seconds, then frowned at Paula.

"Will you be all right by yourself for two minutes? I've got to find the *Regierungsrat* before Hermann gets himself into trouble."

Paula nodded weakly.

Hetzler kicked open the door without trying the knob.

He strode into the house in a fury, then paused, taking in the fireplace, the empty plate on the low table, the old sofa, the space above the hearth. The Enfield was gone. The space where it had hung was noticeably lighter than the wall around it.

He looked at the space above the mantel for a moment, then proceeded with a bit more caution. Before stepping into the bedroom, he cleared his throat. "There's five of us out here," he called. "Give it up now. Make it easy on yourself."

No answer.

He summoned his courage and moved forward. The bed-room was empty, the blanket spilled in a heap on the floor. He moved outside again. Then bent, looking for tracks.

After a minute, he straightened.

"*Schweinehund*," he said to no one, and trotted down the hill toward town.

Chapter Eight

GOTHMUND, LÜBECK

Thomas Brandt walked along the length of the harbor, inspecting the fishing boats moored among the tall reeds, puffing out clouds of smoke that were promptly taken by the wind and dashed.

After reaching the end of the harbor, he turned and began to retrace his steps along the waterfront, moving in the direction of the Fischerweg. Night was falling; along with it came a feeling of pregnant expectation. For some reason, Brandt had a feeling tonight. Soon, he thought, his visitor would arrive.

Just where the feeling had come from, he couldn't say. Possibly the date had something to do with it: only three days shy of the Ides of March. An infamous date; a date with a history. Or possibly it came from somewhere else, from the rustle of the wind or the rhythm of the waves. Brandt's family had been fishermen here at Gothmund for five centuries, and the rhythm of the waves was deeply ingrained in their blood. Sometimes the rhythm seemed to be speaking to him, giving clues about the future.

Superstition, of course. Silly old tales told by bored old fishwives.

But still: he had that feeling.

He hurried a bit faster toward his house. The feeling was strong, and was gaining force by the minute. If his visitor arrived and Brandt wasn't there to meet him, his blackmailers might decide that he had failed to uphold his end of the bargain. Then the other residents of Gothmund might discover the truth about Thomas Brandt. And that was a thought he couldn't bear to face.

Back in his house, he lit a lamp, refilled his pipe, and then set up his easel facing the small window that looked out over the darkening harbor.

He stood in front of the easel for a time, smoking and thinking, without reaching for his brushes. He thought of Noyce, the Englishman who had appeared on his doorstep fifteen years earlier under the guise of an historian researching the Hanseatic League. Brandt had spent a week with Noyce, talking late into the nights over marzipan and strong home-brewed beer, making his memories and scrapbooks available for the man's perusal. Before the week had ended, their relationship had progressed beyond the professional. Then Noyce had vanished back to England; Brandt hadn't heard from him again for eleven years.

One day late in 1936, the letter had appeared.

He remembered the feelings associated with the letter's arrival as clearly as if he had felt them just yesterday. First the guilty excitement, when he had realized the envelope's origin. Then the rush to the lamp, so he could read it with his failing eyes. The way his hands had trembled when he opened it. The sinking feeling of despair as his eyes had moved over the words themselves.

The feeling of utter desolation and betrayal, as he realized that Noyce intended to blackmail him.

Had Noyce always been MI6? Or had he been a scholar, as he had represented himself—another hapless old degenerate, and a victim of blackmail himself? Brandt preferred to think it was the latter. He preferred to think that his relationship with Noyce had been genuine, and that when Noyce had put the screws to him, so to speak, he had done it under duress. But he had no way of knowing for sure.

The letter had informed Thomas Brandt that he was, as of that moment, in the employ of MI6. It had given him a cover address in Lisbon to which he should send his reports, and a list of tasks that he must undertake immediately.

Those early tasks had been slight ones: really just a test, Brandt had soon realized, to see if he could be trusted. He had sent Noyce, as commanded, a prompt reply. In his reply, he had listed the residents of Gothmund, as close to the man as he had been able. He had selected a nearby field that would be appropriate for a secret landing, a harbor that would be appropriate for a secret launch. He had suggested two other men in town who might be vulnerable to blackmail of their own.

For six months, a sort of long-distance dance had occurred between the two men. Eventually, Noyce had become satisfied that Brandt was appropriately under his thumb; and during the same period Brandt had come to understand that Noyce was really only grooming him for future use. If war came again, then the town of Lübeck, situated so near to the coast, could become of vast strategic importance. Until then, Brandt was just another asset, to be cultivated and then set aside.

The final letter had come three years before. According to the letter there was to be no more communication between them. Brandt had become too valuable to risk losing. Instead, he was to wait. At some point, a visitor might arrive, identifying himself as Brandt's cousin. Brandt was to provide sanctuary and deflect any questions raised by the townsfolk. And that was all.

The feeling returned: a nagging premonition.

Tonight, he thought.

But no; he was being fanciful. At his age, one's defenses against fanciful thinking began to crumble. As a child, one believed fantastic things; as a man, one turned away. But with old age the lure of superstition grew again. One wanted to believe there was more, in this world, than what met the eye.

Eventually his mind drifted back further, to more pleasant times. He pictured the town the way it had looked circa 1400, when his family had first settled here. There had been vibrant trade in those days: furs, tars, amber, and honey exchanged for copper, wool, and tin. Those had been the best days for the town, which had recently been given the honor of being declared a free imperial city. These days, by contrast, were not the best days for the town. The honor of free imperial city status had been revoked by the Nazis. Perhaps now the good days of Lübeck were finished forever. Perhaps the days of the Brandt clan were also finished.

Usually, Brandt didn't even bother to wonder about such questions—but he was in a bittersweet mood tonight. The date, he thought. The Ides of March.

His eyes moved back to the blank canvas. A picture occurred to him: the town as it had once been, with its seven church spires rising majestically into the sky and trade flourishing in every corner.

He reached for his brush and began to paint.

PRINZ ALBRECHT STRASSE

When the sun rose, Frick blinked awake.

He had been deep inside a dream—and at first he thought that this was still another part of the dream. An instant before he had been crouching down in the barnyard near Kielce, touching the dancing flame of his lighter to a patch of scrubby brush. Now he was in his office, but he could still hear the cries of the rabble trapped inside the barn, the crackle of fire and the stamping of horses.

But no; the office was real.

He sat up, rubbing at his eyes, and the mundane facts of his surroundings slowly pressed themselves upon him. He had returned to Number 8 Prinz Albrecht Strasse after losing the man's trail by the abandoned Talta. Sat behind his desk long into the night, waiting for the phone to ring. Then taken a catnap on the sofa, using his coat as a pillow—and now it was morning already. The fourteenth of March.

He stood and stretched languorously. His eyes moved to his boots, set on the floor by the sofa, and then to his desk. There they paused, and lingered.

He should have found a way to stay on the front.

Life had been much better there, after all. When a man awoke on the front, the first thing he saw each morning was sky. When he broke his fast, he was fueling himself for meaningful work, active work. And each new day in the field had promised a chance to explore the brave new frontiers of National Socialism, instead of embracing the old ways: the paperwork, the passivity, the waiting.

He scratched absently at one ear, looked away from the desk, and padded to the window. Early sunlight lit the streets, pure and golden. How odd, he thought, that man constructed these concrete canyons in which to contain himself. How odd that man turned away from the lure of nature. It was men who were afraid to truly look within themselves who needed these narrow streets to contain them. . . .

The radiator gave a hissing squeal. He yawned, turned from the window, and groggily left the office to find coffee.

Ten minutes later, he was behind the desk again, trying to make himself concentrate.

The Talta had been deserted not far outside Berlin. And it had indeed contained the Engländer—when Frick had gone there with his dogs, the previous day, they had caught the man's scent. After following the trail for a mile, however, it had abruptly disappeared. Reconstructing the train of events was not difficult. Hobbs had proceeded on foot after leaving the Talta. But he was wounded; he would be in no mood for a vigorous constitutional. And the trail had vanished into thin air. So he had found a car.

But why had no report yet come in?

Because he had killed the driver, Frick thought. So perhaps it was someone who lived alone, who would not quickly be missed. Perhaps—

Someone was looking at him.

His eyes moved up from the desk. They fell on the photograph of his mother. Her eyes, dark and intense, seemed to bore into him. He reached out and turned the frame so that she was looking across the office instead. Then he ran a hand over his mouth, and looked back down at the documents on his blotter.

Someone who lived alone, he thought again, who would not quickly be missed. He decided to assign Hauptmann the task of assembling a list: private car owners who would have reason to travel that remote stretch of road. *Unmarried* private car owners who would have reason to travel that remote stretch of road. Except it was a gargantuan task. There was no guarantee of quick results, and he was loath to wait too long.

There was doubtless a better way to go about the hunt. It was simply a matter of finding it.

He leaned back in his chair. The dream occurred to him again: the whisk of his thumb against the lighter's wheel. The phone rang, and he snatched it to his ear. "Frick," he said.

It was the Wismar *Regierungsrat.* The man had the air of a petty dictator about him; he took his time in explaining himself.

"I have on my desk," the man said, "a copy of a report. I believe it has originated from your office?"

Frick looked at his mother, gazing placidly toward the window, and didn't answer.

"You are searching for a man, yes? An Engländer. We have a description here. Let me see. Heavy build. Hair, light brown. Eyes, light brown. Distinguishing—"

From his voice, Frick could tell many things. The man was a smoker, with a deposit of congestion in his lungs. But there was something worse down there. A sickness. That was what came from living in the environs that man built for himself, he thought. They were filled with poisons. Perhaps the sickness was the reason the man cultivated the air of the petty dictator. He strove to create control, where in reality there was none.

"—in the right leg."

"Yes," Frick said calmly. "That is the man."

"There has been an incident, *Herr Kriminal Inspektor*, in my territory. That is Wismar, of course. But then, I've already told you that."

"Yes," Frick said. "You have."

"The incident occurred just last night. A local woman—her name is Kahr—had given a ride to a man, on her way home from visiting a sister in Berlin. The man fits this description. Heavy build. Hair, light brown. Eyes—"

"Go on," Frick said.

"Let me see. A ride, yes. She found the man on a back road not far outside of Berlin. His car had failed, he claimed. He claimed to be a German. But his command of the language, according to the woman, was weak. He threatened her—forced her to bring him to her home. In Wismar, as I said. That is my territory."

Hauptmann was passing by the open door, holding a breakfast *Käsesemmel* in one hand. Frick snapped his fingers. "Where is the man now?" he asked, waving Hauptmann into the office.

"Ah—hold on a moment, *Herr Kriminal Inspektor*."

A hand covered the telephone; Frick could hear the man talking to someone.

Hauptmann smelled of two kinds of perfume. And below that, his own cologne. Was he cheating on his wife? It seemed a fair conclusion. But how could he think that no one would notice the various scents? Because Hauptmann, like the rest of these men, was living in a world of halftones. Nobody *did* notice these things. They had trained themselves not to.

"Here we are," the *Regierungsrat* said. "The woman managed to escape from the Engländer—but only, I am afraid, after he had taken liberties with her. Now we are not quite certain where he is. But we believe he is on foot. A contingent of brave men have taken it upon themselves to track him. They have been following since last night."

"Moving in what direction?"

"West, *Herr Kriminal Inspektor.* I would be willing—"

Frick hung up the telephone.

"Dogs," he said to Hauptmann, and went to retrieve his Luger from his jacket on the couch.

GOTHMUND

𝕿homas Brandt followed his usual path on his morning walk, inspecting the fishing boats along the harbor as if he might be taking one out himself today, as if his days of fishing were not long in the past. But he moved at a slightly faster clip than usual, for the feeling was still with him—his guest would be arriving soon; if he wasn't there to meet the man, then questions might be raised.

When he neared his cottage again, puffing slightly from the exertion of the walk, he saw Katie Ilgner sitting on the hillock in front of her aunt's house, reading a book with intense concentration. Brandt slowed, hoping to exchange a friendly word. Relations between himself and the Ilgners had been shaky over the past few months, thanks to a series of petty disputes: an incident in which Katie's dog had chewed up Brandt's paintbrushes when he had left them outside overnight, an argument about over-grown devil grass in Brandt's yard, and—most significantly—Frau Ilgner's ever-growing resentment over providing Brandt with hot meals twice a week.

Frau Ilgner had promised her husband, before he had gone off to fight the war, that she would undertake this particular task without complaint. She still brought the meals over on Wednes-days and Sundays, like clockwork, but lately she had offered the plates with a smile so poorly manufactured that it seemed closer to a sneer. She despised Brandt, and he thought that he had a fairly good idea of why this might be so. When Brandt died, his house would become the property of the Ilgners; he had never sired an heir, and the families had been close for generations. But Brandt held on—and on, and on. To Frau Ilgner, his continuing good health must have been a source of frustration. He took endless pleasure in providing this particular aggravation. On the day of his death, he would leave behind few regrets, but one of them would be the knowledge that Frau Ilgner had finally gotten her way.

Katie, a pretty girl of twelve with straw-blond hair that cas-caded down her back, was so deeply immersed in her book that she didn't glance up until Brandt had come within a few feet of her. When she did raise her eyes, her face tightened with nervousness.

"Herr Brandt," she said. "Forgive me, sir. I didn't realize I had . . ."

She looked around, trying to realize what mistake she had made.

Brandt felt himself smiling. Somehow he had become the short-tempered old man of Gothmund, the man whom the children laughed about in private and tried to avoid in public. He wondered what nicknames they had for him. He wondered if there was any point in trying to explain to this girl that he had once been a child himself, that life had a way of making one's face sour, and that, inside, he was still just the same as she was—wanting nothing more than to sit in front of the harbor and read his books or work on his paintings, without fear of harassment.

"Katie," he said. "Don't you look pretty this morning. What are you reading, there?"

She shrugged, and tilted the cover to show him. The title was *The Zaniest Summer*, by Cissy van Marxveldt. "Papa sent it to me," she said.

"Isn't that nice. How is it?"

She shrugged again. "Boring."

"Well, it's good to read anyway. Reading keeps the mind sharp. Even at my age."

"Especially at your age," she said, seemingly without guile.

His smile faded. "Yes," he said. "Especially at my age."

"Are you looking for your cousin? She's inside, having breakfast with Aunt Gerda."

"My . . . cousin?"

Katie nodded toward her aunt's house. "She was knocking on your door for ten minutes."

Brandt licked his lips. "She was, was she?"

"Aunt Gerda says you must not have known she was arriving today. Otherwise you wouldn't have gone on your walk."

"Well," Brandt said. "She is a bit early. Excuse me, Katie, please."

He approached the Ilgner house, his blood hissing through his veins with nervousness. Somehow he had known that his visitor would be arriving today. But he had not expected a woman.

He knocked and then waited. After a moment, the door opened and Frau Ilgner was there, looking at him archly.

"Herr Brandt," she said. "It's not enough for me to keep you supplied with meals, I suppose. It's also my job to look after your cousins, I suppose. Because I don't have enough to keep myself busy, I suppose, without looking after you at every turn."

Brandt only hung his head, and looked past Frau Ilgner to the woman sitting at the breakfast table.

The woman was young—around twenty, he guessed, although he had some trouble judging the ages of young people these days—and pretty, in an unspectacular way, with shoulder-length auburn hair and the fair complexion of a city-dweller. Their eyes met; then she stood, offering a slight curtsy.

"Thomas," she said. "It's so nice to see you again."

She came around the table to embrace him. As her hands closed around his back, she whispered: "Greta."

"Greta," he said. "How wonderful to see you."

"Thank you so much for inviting me. I thought I'd be all right in the city, with Hans gone; but after spending a week by myself, I thought I was losing my mind."

Frau Ilgner was watching them closely.

"You've grown," Brandt said. "A young woman now. The time passes so quickly."

"It does. But you look well, Thomas. Very well."

"Why don't you have a seat," Frau Ilgner said, "and join us for breakfast?"

"Thank you, Frau Ilgner. But we've got too much to catch up on for that. We haven't seen each other for . . . How long has it been?"

"Three years," Eva said.

"Three years! But thank you anyway, Frau Ilgner. Your generosity is most commendable. And thank you for looking after my cousin. The truth is, I wasn't expecting her quite so early."

"We made good time," Eva said. "The trains are running so well these days. And do you know, there's almost no crime at all left in Berlin? It's just remarkable."

"Yes—yes. Well, come along. Do you have any luggage?"

Eva nodded toward a single case resting inside the door. Then she turned to Frau Ilgner. "Thank you so much for your hospitality," she said. "It's so nice to know that people are still friendly, once you get outside of the city."

"How long will you be with us?" Frau Ilgner asked.

"Just for a few days," Eva said airily. "At some point, I'll need to get back to Berlin. My job, you know, won't wait forever. But since Hans went off, the loneliness took me by surprise. It was so kind of Thomas to extend his invitation. . . ."

"Then I'll see you again."

"I hope so." Eva turned back to Thomas and crooked an arm. "Shall we?"

Frau Ilgner watched as they left the house. She kept looking after them for a long minute, her face expressionless. Then she turned away, and began to clear the table.

Eva had achieved such divine distance from reality that she was—against all reason, against all sanity—actually enjoying herself.

When one heard enough bad news, she thought, one slipped away from confronting it. So she had been found out? So she needed to run to an unknown place, to trust a stranger with her life? Why, what fun. At first she hadn't been able to achieve such divine distance. At first—during the night at the rooming house, and all through the long night just passed—she had been taking things all too seriously.

But now she saw things for what they were: a game; a play. All fun, after a fashion. She had found her own theater, here in this remote seaside town. Brandt's small cottage on the Fischerweg looked like a stage set, all deep shadows and too bright colors. She had the feeling that if she could step around a wall quickly enough she would find nothing behind it. It was a façade, constructed entirely for her benefit.

But the fisherman was worried.

He sat at the splintery table and talked—talked endlessly. What had she told the neighbor? The neighbor would be watching them. How long did she plan on staying? How had she gotten here? Were there others coming as well? How many cousins was he expected to have? Noyce had not thought this through, he said. But Noyce was miles away, oceans away, and so he wouldn't have to suffer the consequences. Brandt would be the one to suffer the consequences. Had Noyce made any plan at all?

Eva, who hadn't the faintest idea who Noyce might have been, heard the fisherman out and then answered his questions to the best of her ability. Beneath it all she wanted to reassure him: it was only a game, only a play. He should relax and learn to enjoy it, the way she had.

"I told her we're second cousins. My mother's mother, from Leipzig, was your mother's sister."

"My mother didn't have a sister," Brandt said.

"Does Frau Ilgner know that?"

Brandt shook his head—a gesture of confusion, not an answer.

"I'll be gone in a few days," Eva said. "And yes, someone is meant to meet me here. But I'm not certain if he . . ."

She trailed off. She was not certain if Hobbs had managed to escape after passing her the message, she had been about to say. But it did not seem prudent to tell the old man any more than she needed to. The play into which she had stumbled, after all, wasn't a romance. It was more like a masquerade ball. And when the masks came off, who knew what faces would be revealed?

"I'm not certain if he'll make it," she finished, and left it at that.

Brandt looked at her with his rheumy eyes, then puffed out a coil of smoke. "And how did you get here? Railroad, as you said?"

"No. I had a car."

"Where is it now?"

"I left it outside of town. Don't worry. They won't be able to trace it."

"You're certain?"

"I would say so. It's at the bottom of a pond."

He smoked his pipe again, then resumed talking.

During her time in his home, he said, she was to keep a low profile. Damage had already been done by letting Frau Ilgner see her, but that was nobody's fault but his own. He had not been here to meet her. From now on, however, she was to behave like a U-boat—the vernacular for refugees on the run from the Nazis. She would not leave the house at all until she was leaving for good. She would sleep in the bedroom; he would bring out his old pallet for himself and lay it down here, by the fireplace. If anybody asked, they would stay with the story she had told Ilgner. She was a cousin from Berlin, who had become unexpectedly lonely when her husband had gone off to join the service. She had written Brandt a letter, and he had invited her to come spend a few days in Gothmund. Only to get over the worst of it. She had a job, after all, and they would soon expect her back. And beyond that she was to say nothing.

Eva listened, nodding, still marveling at the divine distance she had achieved.

Thank goodness, she thought, that none of this was real.

Chapter Nine

MECKLENBURG

The bait and switch had failed.

Hobbs knew this for a fact when he came back to the tree with the two flat rocks on either side. This was the landmark he had chosen for himself: the tallest tree in the area, visible from a good distance. If his trick had worked, then there would have been only three sets of tracks around the tree, the ones he had left on his first and second passes and the ones left by his pursuers. But instead he counted four sets. So they had kept his trail, although he had given them bait clear as day—his own footprints heading off through a stretch of muddy earth—and then given them the switch.

He stared at the ground for a long moment. There seemed to be twelve men following him. That was too many by half. Six he could handle—with a good perch to fire from, if he could make certain the sun was behind him. But twelve?

He was beginning to feel quite afraid.

If the bait and switch had failed, then they had a woodsman among them. Which meant that he would need to come up with a better trick.

But he didn't have a better trick.

After staring, he started to move again.

For the first few hours of the chase, when night had still lain across the land, he had not felt especially afraid. He had been high on adrenaline, and optimistic about his chances of shaking the pursuit easily. They were townsfolk, after all, whereas he had spent countless hours in the woods around Surrey during his youth. But now his confidence was flagging. The townsfolk were better trackers than he had assumed. And the leg, which he had barely noticed during the night, had started to give him a fair bit of trouble. For the past hour, he had been using the Enfield as a cane, moving in a clumsy shuffle-step designed to keep as much weight as possible on the rifle.

Yet he still felt a flicker of optimism. This was partly due to the fact that, with the rising of the sun, he had been able to pin down his position. He had studied maps before coming to Germany and now he realized that the Kahr woman had told the truth when she had identified her hometown as Wismar. That meant that he was not so far from Gothmund—which meant that all was not yet lost.

The optimism was also partly due to the Enfield. With the Enfield, he was far from helpless. But a dozen men? Too many.

He would need to wear them down.

The damned leg, he thought. If not for the leg, he could have left them behind by now with sheer speed. But instead he needed to use his brain, and using his brain had never been his strong suit. So what now?

Persistence, of course. During his youth, Hobbs had learned the value of persistence. People rarely had quite as much resistance as they thought they did. And the men following him had less invested in the chase than Hobbs himself.

The first bait and switch had failed. So he would try another.

He moved halfway across a clearing and then carefully retraced his steps. Once he had reached the field's edge, he struck off in a new direction.

He was not tired. He *couldn't* be tired—not yet, not until there were fewer of them. So he was not.

And his leg was not throbbing like a low bass note from a string that never stopped vibrating. He was not famished; his stomach was not trying to eat itself. He was not terrified beyond all rationality. He *couldn't* be these things, or he would have no chance. And so he was not.

Every few minutes, he doubled back. The old tricks, coming from instinct now more than anything else. He wondered where Eva was, if she had managed to escape from Berlin. Why had they been watching her, instead of arresting her? Because they didn't want to arrest her. They wanted her free. As bait? Perhaps.

His mind was not running in a thousand directions at once. He was not on the verge of delirium. His leg was not bleeding again, no matter what his eyes told him.

He misplaced his foot and slipped down into a patch of mud.

Then came to his feet again, growling with fear and frustration. A stitch in his side welled, gave him a few moments of intense pain, and then subsided. He backtracked again. If he stayed within a few miles of town, then his pursuers' desire to give up and go home would be that much stronger. Play on their own weakness. Bait and switch.

Eva was the bait—but what was the switch?

He was coming back, once again, to the tree with the two flat rocks. Please, he thought, let them have given up. Please let there be no fresh tracks by the tree.

But there were. Fewer fresh tracks—but fresh tracks nevertheless.

As he looked at them, the last of his optimism faded. He was left feeling empty, weak, hungry, and very afraid.

Don't give up now, he thought.

No. Because there were fewer tracks. He counted eight, although the elaborate crisscrossing made it difficult to be certain. If he could find the reserves to keep going awhile longer, long enough to find a good perch, to let the sun crest and then drop a bit lower in the sky . . .

Why bother? He was finished. He just hadn't admitted it to himself yet.

For several moments, he let the pessimism flood through him. Then he looked up at the sun, still climbing toward its midday apex. Finished or not, he would do his best to see this through. Because there was something else at stake, wasn't there? He couldn't quite pin it down, but there was something. Something about Eva . . .

A rustling sound caught his attention. In a flash, the rifle was off the ground, trained in the direction of the trees.

The deer who emerged looked at him curiously, then turned and vanished with a flick of its tail.

Hobbs planted the Enfield back on the ground and leaned his full weight on it. He considered smoking a cigarette and decided to save them. A cigarette would make a fine reward, if and when he discouraged the last of the men who had followed him from Wismar.

He struck off again, trying to ignore the fact that his leg was rapidly passing beyond the point of pain, to numbness.

BAYSWATER, LONDON

Arthur Deacon looked up from his comic strip. "Mary," he called. "It's starting."

Lord Haw-Haw repeated his greeting—thanks to his twang, it came out "Jarmany calling, Jarmany calling"—and then launched into a spirited condemnation of the Jewish Communists, backed, as always in his broadcasts, by shadowy Jewish international financiers. Deacon returned his attention to the *Daily Mirror* in his lap. He finished reading his comic strip, paged past an article that failed to catch his interest—deadly serious David Walker—and spent a few moments admiring a photograph of four blank-faced showgirls standing in line. Lovely young ladies, despite their vacant expressions. Ah, if he had still been a single man . . .

Then he realized that Mary had not yet come into the study.

"Mary," he called again. "You're missing it."

He set the paper down and went to check on her.

He had expected she'd be tending to the baby; but as he stepped into the bedroom, he saw that Hugh was in his crib,

143

sound asleep. Mary was sitting before her vanity, going through a try of cosmetics. He went to her and put his hands on her shoulders.

"You're wound tighter than a tourniquet," he said. "Why don't—"

"Shush," she said crisply. "You'll wake Hugh."

He stopped rubbing. After few moments, his hands started to move again, tentatively.

"Do you know," he said, "I thought we could go out on the town tonight. Give your mother a bell, see if she'll come watch the old ankle-biter—"

Mary reached up and pushed his hands off her shoulders.

"I'll take that as a no," Deacon said.

"Bright boy."

"Good. Very good. Brilliant."

He went back to the study, fell into his chair with a flounce, and picked up the newspaper again. He stared at it without seeing. The two rooms separating him from his wife, in reality the length of a single railroad car, felt only slightly smaller than all of King's Cross Station.

She was angry, of course. And for that he couldn't blame her.

When Mary had finally agreed to marry him—on his fourth proposal, by which time he had been desperate—her affirmative had been dependent on a number of conditions. Deacon had agreed to the bulk of them without arguing. He could go without whiskey, late nights, and tobacco, if that was what it took to win her hand. He would even have sworn off food and water, he sometimes thought, if she had insisted on it. For when he had first seen her, it had been like something out of a storybook. For the first time in his twenty-two years, life had suddenly made sense.

It had happened at the cinema. The flick had been *Captain Blood,* starring Errol Flynn. She'd been sitting two rows ahead of him, and as the lights had gone down, she had stretched: a simple stretch. Her hands had touched her hair, lifting it away for a fleeting moment from the back of her neck. And that had been the end of his life as a bachelor, in spirit if not immediately in practice.

For three months following that day, the thought of her neck—so pale and slim, so elegantly arched—had driven him mad. He had begun to haunt the theater, hoping to catch another glimpse of the beautiful girl with the slim pale neck. At that point, oddly enough, he had never even seen her face. But the neck had haunted his dreams; so vulnerable and exposed, so graceful and smooth. When she had finally come back to the theater—the picture that time had been *My Man Godfrey*—he had spent the entire film trying to get up the bollocks to approach her. And approach her he had, once the lights had come up. But he had not been able to put two words together; for she had been as gorgeous from the front as she was from the back.

Somehow, generous heart that she was, Mary had been charmed by his clumsy stammering. For some reason that he still couldn't quite fathom, she had given him his chance. But she had still required convincing. Four proposals' worth of convincing, to be precise, spread out over the course of two years. Finally, she had relented—as long as he obeyed her conditions.

Yet the one condition on which he'd fought was that he give up flying. He had held out on that one until the very day that Hugh had been born. Then a change had come, and his priorities had shifted. One moment he'd been pacing outside the delivery room, grappling with doubt about what he had gotten himself into. He was not a responsible man, after all. He could not look after an entire family. All of it had been a terrible mistake. He had thought this right up until the moment that his eyes had first fallen on Hugh's face; then it was as if a switch had been thrown inside him. He had sworn to leave the RAF and devote himself entirely to his wife and child—and he had not regretted it for a moment.

Until, that was, Oldfield had given him this chance at revenge. Then he had changed his tune. So he couldn't blame her for being angry. But she should have understood, he thought. For the sake of his parents, she should have understood.

He turned two pages, dropped the *Mirror,* and went back to the bedroom.

"Come on, Mary. Don't be that way."

"What way?" she said innocently.

"Well, bloody buggery hell," he said.

This time, upon returning to the study, he left the paper untouched. He went to look out the window at the street. The latest rain was evaporating, giving the air a heavy, charged feeling. Lord Haw-Haw's aristocratic affectations did little to lighten his mood. After a few seconds, he reached out and snapped off the wireless.

After another few seconds, he realized that Mary was standing in the doorway behind him. "Arthur," she said.

"Mm."

"He's fussing."

"Mm."

"He doesn't like it when we quarrel."

He didn't answer.

"You are a very stubborn man," she said. "Do you know that?"

"You are a very stubborn woman," he said.

She had come up behind him; now she began to knead his shoulders. "I do enjoy a good row," she admitted.

"You're as much of a harridan as your mother."

"Fight fair, Arthur."

Now she was turning him around, leaning up for a kiss.

"Go walk your son around the place," she murmured. "See if you can get him back to sleep."

"And if I can?"

"Let's just see what we come up with," she said, "to while away one of our last evenings together."

MECKLENBURG

For the third time in as many minutes, Hermann Hetzler bent to inspect the ground at his feet.

As he prodded at the vegetation, his expression turned querulous. It was a false track—the man had backed up after moving forward, setting his feet in his own prints. The heel section of the track was nearly twice as deep as the toe. But the distinction was less noticeable than it had been the last few times the man had tried the trick. He was learning.

Hetzler stood again. The muscles in the small of his back contracted sharply, making the querulous expression on his face turn pinched. His back was not pleased with all this bending and standing. But the men still with him were losing enthusiasm, so he refrained from reaching around to rub at the muscles. He tried to project strength, confidence, unquestionable assurance.

The men gathered around to hear his verdict.

"He's backtracked again," Hetzler said.

147

He followed the tracks, searching for the place where the man had branched off. He found it in a shallow puddle beside a flat rock. The Britisher had used the water to cover his sidestep; it had devoured the print. Then taken a few steps across the rock, counting on the bright afternoon sun to dry the evidence. Then stepped off again—yes; there. Whatever he was using as a makeshift cane had left a string of dents in the earth, as clear as a trail of bread crumbs. Doubling around behind them, once again.

The circle of faces surrounding Hetzler looked anxious and discouraged. He tried to think of a way to phrase his conclusion without lowering their morale any further. They had spent all night following the man, who was seriously enough wounded that he was using the cane. By these men's estimation, they should have had him by now. But the Engländer had kept his wits. He repeatedly fouled his trail, circling around, staying within a few miles of Wismar. The tactic, Hetzler thought, was designed to foster frustration. And it was working. These men knew only that they had been moving all night and kept coming back to the same place, that a third of their number had already given up. They did not understand that they were drawing steadily closer to their prey.

"Well?" Friedburg demanded.

Hetzler did not look at Friedburg. Instead he looked off into the trees, grandly calculating. "We're close," he said.

"That's what you said an hour ago."

"It was true then. And it's more true now."

"How close?" Ludwig Sturm asked.

"Close."

The men began to mutter among themselves. Hetzler waited, giving them time. The muttering, of course, worked in favor of their quarry. But better for the men to mutter in front of Hetzler than behind his back.

Finally, Friedburg voiced what many of them were thinking: "We should leave it to the Gestapo."

Hetzler shook his head. "Town business," he said firmly, "is town business."

"So you say. But you also say we're close. And it doesn't seem to me as if we're close."

"This is what he wants," Hetzler answered. "He's counting on this. Why else would he keep circling back?"

More low muttering. Hetzler looked from one face to another, trying to gauge the loyalties. Nearly half of the group, he thought, were on Friedburg's wavelength. The other half understood better. They looked dispirited, but still willing.

"My feet hurt," Friedburg said.

"As do mine," Hetzler said. "But not half as much as his must."

"How do you know these are his tracks at all? For all I know, you're leading us on a wild-goose chase."

Hetzler didn't justify that with an answer.

For five minutes more, the men talked. Again Hetzler waited. Let them get the grousing out of their systems, he thought. Let the ones who were going to turn back do it now, so that the rest of them could continue without interference.

At last, a man named Horst took the lead. "Hermann," he said. "I've had enough. Leave it to the Gestapo."

Hetzler didn't argue.

"Horst is right," another said. "For all we know, the man's gone."

Hetzler waved a hand. "Go, then."

The group separated like quicksilver flowing down a pane of glass. When the naysayers had gone, Hetzler saw that only five remained: himself, Sturm, the farmboy Messel, the blacksmith Grünewald, and—astoundingly—Friedburg.

Friedburg looked defensive.

"Go with them," Hetzler said impatiently, "if that's what you want."

"But you say we're close."

"We are."

"So I'll stay."

Hetzler controlled himself. The man liked complaining more than anything else. If he went back to town, he could no longer complain. So he would stay—in all likelihood, dragging the rest of them down with him, to the best of his ability.

He put Friedburg from his mind and turned back to the tracks on the ground.

"We can move faster with five," he said. "It won't be long now. If you can't keep up, you'll be left behind."

None of the men answered. After a few seconds, Hetzler chose a direction. He struck off without looking back.

Chapter Ten

Hauptmann and Bandemer were almost useless, Frick thought.

The road was ending in a thick snarl of underbrush. Hauptmann eased the Mercedes to a stop, then made a sound of aggravation. *Useless*, Frick thought again.

"We can't make it through that," Hauptmann said. "Should we clear the road? . . ."

Confusion and frustration seeped through his every pore, reeking. Frick shook his head. "Wait here," he said.

He left the car, stepping out into the wild and breathing deep.

There were so many answers, to be told by the air and the trees and the grass. He became immediately aware of a ballet that had been going on for several hours already, a few hundred yards to the east. He strode off in that direction, leaving the men and the dogs in the car behind him.

Here—a spoor that crossed back on itself. The grass was bent, pressed in countless directions, stippled with regular indentations. He closed his eyes and opened the rest of himself. The man had been leading them on a merry chase, he thought. The man was a worthy opponent. And these others who were chasing him were mongrels, as ineffectual as the men waiting for him back in the Mercedes.

He held very still, letting himself feel the truth. What came was not precisely truth, but a humming instinct. Over the next ridge, he thought. That was where he had to go.

He went, his eyes barely open, moving very slowly.

Another pretzel of tracks, scents, and clues. When they had passed this place—many minutes after they had been at the first site—the Engländer had still been in control. Playing a game, Frick thought; wearing down his pursuers. And his strategy had been effective. Now the men on his trail were half their previous number.

But his footsteps were deeper, more labored; the indentations were so pronounced that groundwater was visible near the bottoms. Fatigue was taking its toll. And was there blood, coming from the man's wound? There was. He couldn't see it and he couldn't smell it; but he could sense it. Dark blood; granular blood. The blood was . . . there.

He found it.

And where had they gone then?

Back over their own trail again. Behind them, and farther to the east.

Instead of following farther, he went back to the car.

"Bandemer," he said to the man in the backseat. "Let me have the dogs."

The door opened; the leashes were handed out. Frick led the three dogs back to the second site. He could feel Hauptmann and Bandemer following hesitantly behind him, baffled. Frick relocated the Engländer's trail, then knelt beside it. The dogs clustered around, rooting in the grass.

He watched. They were still better than him, he thought. They were made for this.

Yet they lacked reason. Once they had caught the man's scent, they tried to follow it literally, just as the man's pursuers had done. But Frick tugged at the leashes, to let them know that something else was required. A leap of imagination; a glimpse into the quarry's mind. He chose the direction that felt most right, and followed it.

Suddenly, one of the dogs—the small, vicious one—was pulling strongly to the left.

Frick let him pull. Soon the others had caught the same trail. Then Frick caught it himself. When they came upon the tracks, they were still fresh. A drop of blood the size of a large beetle was clinging to a blade of grass. He bent and touched it. Still wet. They were not far behind, now.

They would need to leave the car, and follow on foot.

Hauptmann and Bandemer were trotting up behind him. He handed the leashes back to Bandemer. "This way," he said. "We must abandon the car."

"*Herr Kriminal Inspektor*—how can you be sure?"

He considered trying to explain his instincts, decided it would be a waste of breath. "I trust the dogs," he said instead. "Do you not?"

"Well . . ."

"If you'd rather wait for us here, Herr Hauptmann . . ."

"Of course not. I will come along."

Frick kept the contempt he felt off his face. The man was weak, conflicted; a fool. He did not trust himself.

But the Engländer was better. *A worthy opponent*, he thought again.

They headed off, half-running to keep up with the straining dogs.

GOTHMUND

Eva watched the old man's back as he painted.

His body was wider through the hips than through the shoulders. The material of his shirt constricted with each fluid movement of the brush across the canvas, showing that peculiar pear-shaped body in sharp relief. It was a curious phenomenon, she thought. After almost forty-eight hours spent in the little house with nothing to look at, it seemed all the more curious still.

Then she pressed her hands against each other, and tried to find something else to distract her.

Her eyes moved from the pallet to the fireplace to the table and then back to the old man at the easel. The painting on which he worked was not bad at all: the bay through the window as it must once have looked, with old-fashioned boats moored against a pastel dock and seven jeweled church spires rising in the foreground. Similar paintings adorned the cottage walls, mostly variations on the same theme: Germany as it had once been, the Germany of tradition.

She stood, stifling a yawn. Only one more day, she thought. Then she would be out of here—on her way back to England.

Except that Hobbs had not yet arrived.

And so she did not know the precise location of the extraction site.

An airplane, the letter had said, would meet them north of Gothmund. But was it an airplane or a seaplane? And how many possible landing sites were in the vicinity? She could ask the fisherman. Perhaps he would have her answers. But if she showed her helplessness, she would be putting her fate into his hands— even more securely into his hands than she already had. And if he sensed that things had gone terribly wrong—Hobbs had never arrived; the operation was in jeopardy, if not in ruins—he might even turn on her. It seemed that from the old man's perspective it would be far easier to turn her in to the Gestapo than to risk staying involved with a shattered operation.

But he was doing this for a reason, she thought. The British had not chosen him at random. She would need to trust the judgment of MI6, and trust that the fisherman would not betray her even after she revealed her need for help. She had no other choice.

She went to stand behind him.

"You don't need to watch over my shoulder," he said.

"I'm sorry. I have a question."

He said nothing to encourage her to continue. The brush in his hand moved to the paints, dipped, swirled, and moved back to the canvas.

"The man who was meant to meet me here," Eva said. "If he doesn't arrive, then I don't know where they're supposed to fetch me."

"They?"

"The airplane."

"Ah," he said. "The airplane."

"Yes."

"Has this been arranged in advance?" Brandt asked. "It hardly seems like it."

"My friend was meant to meet me here," Eva said, trying to keep the edge out of her voice.

"I've gathered that."

"But if he doesn't—and if you can't help me—then I won't be able to leave."

The brush paused in mid-stroke.

"And I don't think you'd enjoy that," she said. "Would you?"

"No," he said. "I don't think I would."

"So I need your help."

Brandt looked at his canvas for a moment more. Then he sighed, added a final corkscrew of red, and set his paints on the plankboard floor.

As they left the house, Eva saw the neighbor Katie Ilgner sitting with her book in front of the harbor. Something about the way the girl was bent over the pages, her brow deeply furrowed, struck her as familiar. But Katie didn't look up as they strolled casually past her, arm in arm, and Eva soon found her mind turning elsewhere.

Brandt led her along the length of the bay, then came to an abrupt stop. He turned to a rough-hewn path that led up a small wooded hill. "Such a beautiful day," he said cynically. "Do you feel up to walking a little farther?"

Eva bowed. "After you."

They began to negotiate the primitive path. For about ten minutes, they walked without speaking, gaining altitude; Eva could hear the man's breath coming harder. Finally, they reached a clearing perhaps eighty feet wide and four times as long. On three sides, the field was surrounded by trees. On the fourth, the land sloped down to a small stagnant lake the color of limes.

"If it's to be an airplane," Brandt said, "it will be here."

Eva looked around dubiously. "It seems awfully small," she said.

"It is the location I supplied to Noyce. Unless something else has been arranged . . ."

"Can a plane really land here?"

"For both of our sakes—let us hope so."

They looked at the field for another few moments. Then Eva shrugged, and they began to retrace their steps along the path. For several minutes, she concentrated on placing her feet, trying to avoid the tangles of brush and thistles. At length, Brandt asked conversationally, "So it's to be tomorrow?"

"I think so. Yes."

"What time?"

"Tomorrow. That's all I know."

"And what am I to do if your friend arrives after you've gone?"

She shrugged again.

Brandt didn't speak for another two minutes. As they were drawing close to the bay and the air took on the tang of saltwater, he said, "Give Noyce a message for me, when you get back."

Eva considered telling him she didn't know Noyce, then decided there was no point. "All right," she said.

"Tell him he's gotten all he's going to get from me. I'm finished."

"All right."

"The next time a 'cousin' appears on my doorstep, he'll find the door locked."

"I'll pass it along," she promised.

When they reached his house on the Fischerweg, the girl was still sitting by the bay, still absorbed in her book. The feeling of familiarity took Eva again. Young Katie Ilgner reminded her of something—or of someone.

Then she had it. Of course; the girl reminded her of Eva herself. Herself as she once had been, sitting outside the barn with her nose buried in a book as the horses nickered importantly from nearby stables.

She felt a sudden, irrational urge to run to the girl, rip the book from her hands, and fling it into the water.

Brandt noticed her eyes on the girl. He elbowed her sharply. "Inside," he said.

Eva tore her eyes away, and followed him inside.

Frau Ilgner watched Brandt and Eva as they stepped through the door. Then she turned to the man standing beside her: Karl Baumbach, the local *Regierungsrat*.

"You see," Frau Ilgner said. "That is the first time they've left the house since she arrived."

Baumbach nodded sagely. "Mm," he said.

"A cousin, we're supposed to believe? There's no family resemblance. None whatsoever."

Baumbach nodded again. "Although sometimes," he said, "cousins don't look very much alike."

"My Nana knew his mother for years. They grew up together. She didn't have a sister."

"Mm."

"He's up to something," Frau Ilgner said.

"You may be right."

"Well? What are you going to do about it?"

Baumbach looked out the window for a few more seconds. Then he raised his chin an inch, and tightened the muscles in his cheeks.

"I will place a call," he said.

Chapter Eleven

MECKLENBURG

Hermann Hetzler paused, sneering into the low-hanging sun. The land here was open, a series of gentle swells, with only the burned-out ruins of the old Scheppel place breaking the integrity of the horizon. Either the man had vanished for a moment behind one of the gentle swells—in which case he would show himself momentarily as he continued moving—or he had taken refuge in the dilapidated hulk of the Scheppel house.

Close, Hetzler thought. *Very close now.*

Ludwig Sturm, standing beside Hetzler with his old Mauser rifle in one hand, was also looking thoughtfully at the ruins of the house. Around them, the other three men waited, stooped from exhaustion.

"What do you think?" Hetzler asked.

Sturm didn't hesitate. "He's there."

They moved forward again, over land that squelched softly. As they drew nearer, the sun needled Hetzler's eyes, blinding him. He raised his hand; the men piled to a stop around him.

"See how the sun glares," Hetzler said. "That's not by chance."

"An ambush," Sturm said.

Hetzler squinted for another few seconds. Then he turned to Friedburg, who was looking dolefully at his feet.

"We'll surround him," Hetzler said. "He'll try to move again when night falls. Then we'll take him."

The men murmured agreement—all except Friedburg, whose face registered annoyance. "Who put you in charge?" he asked.

Hetzler gave no answer, looking instead to see the other men's reaction to the question. He saw nothing that troubled him. Sturm was already beginning to move off, around to the right of the Scheppel place. Messel, a mountainous farmboy with enough muscles to make up for his lack of wits, was busy inspecting the tines of his pitchfork. Grünewald was checking his rifle.

Friedburg saw that he stood alone. He sighed in defeat; then his eyes found Grünewald's. They began to move off together around the opposite side of the house from Sturm.

Hetzler turned to Messel. "Tired?" he said.

Messel nodded.

"Never fear. As soon as—"

Then a shot rang out, and the words caught in his throat.

.   .   .

The old Enfield was puckish; it dragged.

Hobbs pressed his lips together, and tried to judge what had happened.

The shot had gone wide—to the right, he thought. He swung the barrel a few degrees to the left and looked down the lustrous metal. The sight landed just past the first man who had broken from the group. He was obviously trying to flank Hobbs, but he hadn't yet reached the shallow depression that might shelter him; he was out in the open.

Hobbs took a second before firing again, to make certain everything was in order. His right thumb extended over the rifle stock, creating a spot weld between cheek, hand, and gun. They were a single unit, he and the gun. His eyes flicked up to the trees a quarter-mile distant. He estimated the wind from their lazy motion, and compensated by moving the barrel another fraction of an inch. Just like the days back in Surrey, he thought, duck hunting with his mates.

He held his breath and squeezed the trigger again. This time he was rewarded by a squeal of pain.

He worked the bolt.

The man he had hit was down, and motionless. For the moment, Hobbs left him alone. He swung the sight back toward the others. The two who had been heading in the opposite direction had hit the ground; they were huddling down in the tall grass. In time, they would need to move again. They would make better targets then. As long as he didn't let them get past him, behind the house . . .

He sighted on the last two, the two standing farthest away.

One held a pitchfork; the other was shielding his eyes against the glare. But both were still standing at full height. Out of range. Or were they?

He sighted, compensated for the Enfield's drift, compensated for the wind, then raised the barrel by instinct—feeling the arc of the bullet—and fired again.

He missed, but evidently not by much; both men were suddenly pressing themselves flat against the ground. He worked the bolt again.

Silence.

He could take another try at the nearer two on the ground. But why waste the ammunition? The men were pinned. If he could hold them there until dark, he could slip away.

On the other hand, he would rather finish it now.

He lowered the rifle. The pack of Player's, propped on a crumbled ledge of brick beside the spare magazines, caught his eye. Only two cigarettes remained. He should save them. He should concentrate on what was going on in front of him.

The nearer pair on the ground were moving again—rising into unwieldy crouches, trying to circle around the back of the ruined house.

He socketed the gun back into his shoulder, and took careful aim.

Friedburg's feet hurt.

He tried not to think about it. He kept waddling forward, peering from time to time in the direction of the burned-out house. Each time he looked up, the sun drilled mercilessly into his eyes. Beside him, Grünewald was moving in the same awkward crab-walk, torn between staying low and traveling fast. *A good policy*, Friedburg thought. He should try to get a little lower himself. Yet his mind was fixed on his feet—they hurt.

A moment later, Grünewald had smacked him in the face with the stock of his rifle.

At first Friedburg couldn't understand why Grünewald had done this. Because he had slept with the man's sister? That must have been it. But how did Grünewald know about that? Besides, it was ancient history. Why now, of all times?

He put a hand to his forehead. The hand came away red, far redder than it should have been from a single blow. Then he understood—Grünewald had not smacked him at all. He had been shot.

The rifle cracked again, and a white-hot poker speared him in the chest.

Friedburg fell onto his back. The poker withdrew and ice water flooded in to replace it; there seemed to be no air in his lungs. He could see Grünewald's face looming in his vision, concerned. Friedburg tried to open his mouth, to tell the man that he was all right. It was only a flesh wound. The bullet had only grazed him. The real problem was with his feet. His feet ached like the devil.

A moment later, he was gone.

Grünewald checked the man's pulse with two fingers on his throat. Then he turned back to the house, hefting the rifle in his hand. He couldn't see anything but sun.

He rose to his feet and charged forward.

Hobbs worked the bolt again.

One round left in the magazine. And now one of the men was

making a break for it, running at top speed. Hobbs led him, aiming off. He fired.

Missed.

The man ducked around the side of the house, out of his field of vision.

He bit down a curse and jammed a fresh magazine into the gun, keeping his eye on the other three. The first one he had hit was still lying motionless. *Not dead*, he thought with sudden certainty; *playing possum.* The second, however, was not acting. Even from here, Hobbs could make out the bubbling chest wound, the slow river of blood staining the grass beneath him. The last two were still huddled against the ground, out of range.

He raised the Enfield again.

The one that had gotten past him might pose a problem. But for the time being he couldn't afford to worry about that. If he let his attention lapse, he would have even more problems.

He aimed at the one who was playing possum. Compensated. He fired, and the man's body jumped like a sandbag hit by a hard wave.

Now the last two began to move forward, splitting up. Trying to buy time, he thought, for the one who had gotten behind him.

He couldn't stay in his perch any longer—not with the man behind him, between him and the setting sun. He carefully slung the Enfield back over his shoulder, then picked up the magazines and the cigarettes and stuffed them into the satchel. Then he began to shimmy back along the rafter, toward the stairs.

The wind picked up, wailing mournfully through the valley, fighting with the trees on the horizon.

Hobbs had backed halfway toward the stairs when the rafter beneath him groaned, buckled, and split.

. . .

Grünewald saw him: lying on an exposed beam on the second floor, facing out to the field.

Grünewald was rusty with the rifle. But he would overcome the rustiness. He was a blacksmith; precision was his business. He would place a bullet squarely in the man's spinal column above his shoulder blades, incapacitating him instantly. The Engländer would not even squeeze the trigger reflexively, as his muscles contracted at the instant of death, to take a last shot at whomever he had in his sights. He would collapse as if poleaxed. A difficult shot; but he would manage it. For Paula.

He sighted on the back of the man's head, then dropped the barrel a quarter of an inch. Above the shoulder blades but below the brain stem. He would have only one chance . . .

Then the man was moving.

Shimmying back, momentarily hidden behind a slab of timber. Grünewald swore roughly. He had missed his chance. He swept the rifle to the right, to the head of the exposed staircase, and tried to clear his mind. He would have another shot in a moment. And now that the man was no longer aiming out at the field, he would not need to hit the spinal column just so. Any shot would do. In a second, the man would appear again. Grünewald held the rifle motionless. Any second now . . .

The wind picked up; the beam on which the man was lying groaned, low and long—and then snapped, spilling the man down to the first floor in a shower of debris.

Grünewald blinked owlishly. The rifle swung down to the first story, but found no target; only a pillowy cloud of dust and grit. In a moment, the wind would sweep it away. Then he would have his target. The foreigner was probably stunned by his fall, perhaps even unconscious. Perhaps they could bring him back to town in one piece and take their time with him.

He moved forward, peering cautiously into the cloud of dust.

There—no. Only a shattered beam. There—to the left, half-pinned under a splintered rafter. But all he could see was a rifle.

The rifle spoke, curtly.

Grünewald fell back, a freshet of blood pumping from his throat.

Hermann Hetzler stopped moving.

The sun was lower now—a crucial few degrees lower. For the first time, he could clearly see the tableau before him. And it was not encouraging.

To his right lay Sturm, either dead or dying. A few paces ahead and two dozen to his left lay Friedburg. Friedburg was on his back, his limbs splayed loosely, his chest oozing gore. His days of complaining were finished.

An ambush, Hetzler thought. He had known it. And yet they had walked right into it.

Messel was still moving forward, his head bowed low like a bull's, the pitchfork his only weapon. Too stupid to know what he was doing, Hetzler thought. Well, perhaps he had the right idea. God looked out for idiots and children. But Hermann Hetzler was neither—and he had no desire to die.

Suddenly, leaving the man to the Gestapo seemed like not such a bad idea at all.

But Grünewald was back there, behind the house. Perhaps Grünewald would have some luck. He tried to make himself move again, but fear had taken him in a firm grip. He only stood, conscious that he should keep walking, unable to do it.

The wind gusted; then something happened in the house, creaking and cataclysmic. A great cloud of dust rose, obscuring the rays of the sun.

Hetzler stood for one more second, trying to find some hidden reserve of courage.

Then he gave up, turned on his heel, and fled.

Hobbs was listening to the bells.

The bells were coming from all around him, reverberating. He inhaled and got a lungful of dust, then coughed it viciously back out. When the coughing had passed, his mind felt marginally clearer. He was surrounded by rubble, broken brick, half-mulched wood. The beam, he realized. The beam had collapsed.

He groaned, and tried to sit up.

A broken rafter was pinning him. As he looked at it, he realized with a small jolt of surprise that the satchel was still in his hands. The rifle was still on his back. He reached for it, but couldn't find the leverage to pull it free. He tried again, to no effect.

The bells in his head grew louder; he swooned. They softened and he came awake again. There was no pain. Only a feeling of terrible urgency. How many men were left?

Another fit of coughing took him. When it was past, the feeling of urgency receded, replaced by a sense of unnatural tranquillity. He had been in worse situations, he thought. He couldn't recall them at the moment; but they had happened, and he had survived them. So he would survive this.

Then he grinned. He was conning himself—or trying to, in any case.

He found himself looking at the strap across his chest. A moment later, his eyes moved to a sharp splinter of wood jutting from the broken rafter. He looked back and forth several times before his mind caught up to his eyes. Then he rearranged himself, inching his torso closer to the timber. The leather strap caught on the sharp edge of wood—just so. He worked a hand free and painstakingly pulled the leather tight against the jagged beam. Worked it back and forth. After a few seconds of sawing, the strap began to separate.

Then it snapped, and the rifle came loose. He pulled the Enfield around into his lap. He craned his head, looking outside of the rubble, trying to figure out what came next.

A man was there—a scant dozen feet away. Peering into the debris, a rifle held at his shoulder.

Hobbs planted the stock of the Enfield against his hip. He aimed the best he could, one-handed, and then fired. A wild shot. But a good one; the man fell away, out of sight.

A hiss came from between his teeth. *Cocksucker*, he thought. *Almost had me. Didn't you?*

But he wasn't done yet, God damn it. After watching for a moment to make sure the man was not going to rise again, he turned his attention back to the rafter. There would be no way to do this gently. So he did it harshly—in one wrenching tug, ignoring the sudden flare of pain, ignoring the strip of flesh that was peeled from his calf.

He dragged himself through the settling grit, onto damp grass. The man he had shot was lying here, dying. Hobbs glanced at him for a moment, then looked away. He tried his leg. It blazed with agony.

Eva, he thought.

The ringing in his ears rose again, deafening.

Messel rounded the corner of the house, pitchfork in hand.

There were two men lying on the ground within a dozen feet of each other. Neither moved; both, he thought, were unconscious. Then he moved to Grünewald and realized that the man was not unconscious but dead. His face was china-pale; his eyes stared bleakly into oblivion.

Messel looked down at the blacksmith for a few seconds. Then he moved to check on the Engländer.

This one was still alive—swimming in and out of awareness, his eyes coated with a milky cataract of confusion. The Enfield lay near one limp hand. Messel pushed it away with his foot, almost leisurely. As the broken strap trailed across the man's arm, his eyes sharpened, flashing with panic.

He was right to panic, Messel thought coldly.

Hobbs was trying to speak, but he didn't have the air. Instead he made a liquid sound, frantic but thin. *A rapist*, Messel thought with a curl of his lip. *A rapist and a murderer.*

He raised the pitchfork to deliver the fatal stroke.

He never saw the man who came up behind him and fired a bullet into the base of his skull.

Hauptmann had been opening his mouth to call a command— but Frick had moved too quickly for that.

Now the boy he had shot was headless, sprawled on the ground like a half-assembled mannequin. It had not been necessary to shoot the boy, Hauptmann thought. A warning would have sufficed. But Frick had not given him the opportunity. If that was what time on the front did to a man, then Hauptmann would be happy never to experience that honor. He would rather sit in his office, flipping through papers, and let others learn the harsh lessons of combat. That way, at least, he could sleep at night.

He did not expect to sleep well tonight—if he did manage to find a chance to lie down—after seeing the corpses that littered the ground around them.

Frick did not seem burdened by any such thoughts. He approached the farmboy and rolled him away with one booted foot. The farmboy, despite the fact that part of his head was gone, was still alive. Frick raised the gun again. His finger tightened on the trigger—yet nothing happened.

He looked at the Luger dispassionately. Then he looked back at the farmboy. Now life was fleeing; the eyes darkened. Frick stuffed the Luger back into its holster, and knelt down beside the Engländer.

When he turned from the man, his face was a study of equanimity.

"Hauptmann," he said calmly. "Go and fetch the car. Bring it as far as the road allows. Leave the dogs with the *Regierungsrat*. We'll meet you in a half hour."

Hauptmann nodded jerkily, and turned. He nearly bumped into Bandemer, who was holding the dogs on leashes and staring at the scene before him with an expression of horror.

Bandemer's red-rimmed eyes glanced toward Hauptmann, but Hauptmann refused to meet them. He grabbed for the leashes and then hurried off in the direction of town.

Frick had returned to the man on the ground. The prisoner was only half-conscious; his head lolled loosely on his shoulders.

As Bandemer watched, Frick smiled at the prisoner—an oddly tender smile. Then he sensed Bandemer watching him, and the smile fell away.

He stood, tugging his uniform straight.

"Give me a hand," he said. "And wipe that look off your face. You embarrass yourself."

Chapter Twelve

The Bentley was heading into Sussex.

Oldfield waited until Deacon had asked, then explained that they would be making a quick stop on their way to the airfield. The Prime Minister wanted to give Deacon some last words of wisdom.

"Just stand there and nod, old boy, and don't make a fuss. Chamberlain's under enough pressure these days. The last thing he needs is some smart-aleck pilot arguing with him. All right?"

Deacon shrugged, and nodded.

They came to an eighteenth-century estate set in a deer park, passed through a tall gate, and then drove for what seemed like miles past manicured gardens and terraced lakes.

The heart of Plumpton Place was a sprawling mansion surrounded by a gothic moat. A row of dark sedans was parked outside the house. Inside, Deacon and Oldfield were escorted to a sunny drawing room, then announced by an extremely short butler with lifts in his shoes.

But Chamberlain was already involved in a discussion; for the first few minutes of their visit, he ignored them completely. They stood just inside the doorway, hands folded patiently, waiting.

The man with whom Chamberlain was talking was Winston Churchill, the First Lord of the Admiralty. And Churchill, as usual, was on a tear.

"The time for keeping up appearances," he was saying, "is past. It is time to act, Mr. Prime Minister, and appearances be damned. If we hesitate much longer, our last chance will be lost."

Chamberlain was already shaking his head. The man's age, Deacon thought, seemed to have caught up to him almost without warning. His graying hair looked thinner than it had in newsreels taken just a few months before; loose rolls of skin had appeared under his chin. And the way he held his hands—one tightly entwined in the other—gave the impression of a man trying hard to control himself, perhaps even trying to mask a tremor. But it was not surprising that age had finally caught up to Chamberlain. Hitler had thrown too many lies in his face, and violated too many promises, for the Prime Minister to deceive himself any longer. He was being forced to face the truth—that he had led England into an untenable situation; that in today's world, goodwill and a desire for peace were not nearly enough.

Churchill, in contrast, was brimming with energy. As he spoke, his immense cheeks quavered, his hands moved to illustrate his words, and his eyes glittered ferociously.

"Without iron ore from Sweden, Mr. Prime Minister, Germany will be crippled. Eleven million tons flow every year down the Gulf of Bothnia, then across the Baltic. But in wintertime, ice blocks the shipping route; the ore must be transported by rail to Navrik, then shipped via the coast to Germany. Hitler is depending on our respecting Norwegian neutrality to ensure the safety of these shipments. For all of the winter just past, we have played into his hands—but it may not be too late to correct our mistake."

"I will not be the one to violate the neutrality of Norway," Chamberlain pronounced.

"Mr. Prime Minister, will Hitler respect their neutrality for a minute longer than it suits his purpose? When it comes time—"

"Our interference is precisely what he desires. It will supply him with a pretext to invade."

Churchill could not conceal his exasperation. "Hitler will take Norway if and when he chooses, regardless of our actions. If we do not supply the pretext within his schedule, then he will supply one himself. But there is still a chance to block the crucial shipments of ore. We must mine the Norwegian Leads."

"That would be a gesture of open hostility."

"Toward a country that is already at war with England, Prime Minister."

"We are not at war with Norway," Chamberlain said resolutely. "And we would need to dispatch a force to Navrik, to ensure the success of the operation. In the judgment of the world, we would be guilty of naked aggression—"

"I have discussed the situation with the War Cabinet," Churchill interrupted. "They are in complete agreement with me. The time for keeping up appearances is past."

For a moment, Deacon thought that Chamberlain would take

the First Lord of the Admiralty to task for his audacity; but then the Prime Minister's posture slackened. In that moment, he looked like a saddened old man besieged on all sides, who had lost confidence not only in those who surrounded him but also in himself.

Chamberlain shook his head again, as if trying to shake away his doubts. His eyes darted evasively. Then he glanced up and seemed to see Oldfield and Deacon for the first time. He seized on their presence with an enthusiasm that struck Deacon as somewhat manufactured: an excuse to avoid continuing the conversation with Churchill.

"Mr. Oldfield!" he said brightly. "Now, here we have a fine fellow, Mr. Churchill. Mr. Oldfield is here to direct the war against our enemies, instead of against our prospective allies. He is Director General, you know, of MI6."

Churchill puffed out his cheeks with frustration, but summoned the courtesy to nod his head.

"And this must be the young pilot," Chamberlain said. "Deacon, is the name?"

"Arthur Deacon," Oldfield said. "The pride of the RAF, and as fate would have it, my favorite nephew."

Chamberlain absorbed Deacon with his hazy brown eyes. "Why is it," he asked, "that all pilots have this look about them?"

Deacon blinked. "What look is that, Mr. Prime Minister?"

"Never mind, Mr. Deacon. Thank you for stopping by. I hoped to take the opportunity to impress upon you the import of your mission."

"I am quite aware of it, Mr. Prime Minister."

"I may have misjudged the little Austrian corporal. But

thanks to the efforts of men like yourself and Mr. Oldfield, all is not yet lost."

Churchill, who had moved to inspect a globe in a corner of the drawing room, muttered something to himself. Chamberlain ignored it.

"We may have a slight advantage in numbers," the Prime Minister continued. "Four million men in our combined armies, as compared to the Germans' three. Yet our armored divisions are not battle-ready, and we suffer a dearth of trained reserve troops. The intelligence that we seek is therefore of great interest to the War Council."

"I will do my very best, Mr. Prime Minister, to retrieve it for you."

"Very good. I know that you will."

He turned back to Churchill.

"Mr. Churchill," he said. "Regretfully, I cannot continue arguing the matter at this time. I require rest."

Churchill bristled.

"Perhaps a nap," Chamberlain said. Now he was looking off into the parlor with a wistful air. "If you insist on continuing, I will make time this afternoon."

"Mr. Prime Minister," Churchill said. "If you are not up to the demands of leading our nation in this most desperate hour—"

Oldfield was tugging on Deacon's sleeve, pulling him toward the doorway. "That's it?" Deacon whispered.

Oldfield nodded.

They moved outside, back into the Bentley, then down the winding road that led away from the mansion. Oldfield did not seem interested in discussing the Prime Minister's words. He was looking out the window, his brow creased in thought. There was a sadness about him now, Deacon thought. After spending time in Chamberlain's company, he felt a touch of sadness himself. The man's fatal flaw had been optimism; and that optimism had led him to ruin.

Chamberlain, and perhaps the rest of the world.

And now the best chance of averting disaster lay in Deacon's hands.

He wished he'd found time for a last drink before leaving Bayswater.

Part Three

Chapter Thirteen

The man called Frick was talking.

Hobbs was conscious of the voice only in fits and starts, as a conversational rising and ebbing. He couldn't tell whether the words were addressed to him, to the driver, or to the stocky man sitting in the passenger-side seat—the one they called Hauptmann. Since they were in English, he supposed they were addressed to him, or were at least for his benefit.

But the words made little impression; most of his mind was occupied with his leg. The wound there had opened again during his run, and the torn material of his trousers had become intertwined with tatters of bloodied bandage. As he looked at it, a sense of dislocation washed over him. That was his leg, looking like a half-chewed piece of meat. Impossible.

"The Russians," Frick was saying, "are not quite as worthless as some might think. They are animals—but as such they have a certain animal cunning."

The Mercedes was on a road that was not quite a road, leading ever deeper into thickly wooded hills. A canopy of branches closed above them as they drove, blocking out the starlight. Just what their destination was, Hobbs didn't know. Following his capture, they had returned to Wismar and dropped off the dogs; he had assumed that he would be transferred somewhere for interrogation. But Frick seemed to have a plan of his own, and the other two were evidently as in the dark about the details as Hobbs himself.

"And a certain foolish bravery," Frick went on. "They play a remarkable game, the Russians. It originated during the Great War, I understand, somewhere in Rumania. A group of czarist officers found themselves with too much time and not enough food. So they removed a cartridge from the cylinder of a gun, spun it, put it to their heads, and pulled the trigger. The chances were six to one that it meant certain death. But that was the intention, of course. Once one man was dead, there was more food for the rest."

His tone was casual, the tone of a man discussing a fine night at the opera.

"Tall tales," Hauptmann sniffed. "Nobody is so crazy. Not even the Russians."

"Perhaps," Frick said. "Or perhaps not. In either case—the game intrigues me. I would very much like to see it played with my own eyes. Do you suppose, *Herr Kriminal Assistant*, that you might stage a demonstration for me?"

The stocky man up front laughed nervously.

"You and the Engländer might challenge each other," Frick

continued. "We will play the safer version. All of the chambers are emptied except one. Then, you see, the chances of survival are higher. The game lasts longer."

"*Herr Kriminal Inspektor*, if you don't watch out, you'll get the reputation for being the funny one."

"Ah," Frick said. "Aha. Yes."

Then they were entering a small clearing; Hobbs could hear the trickle of water in a nearby brook, the susurrous rustle of leaves. The moon overhead, almost full, peeked through narrow spaces between the branches.

The driver twisted the keys; the engine fell silent. For a few moments, nobody spoke.

"So," Frick said then. "Would you like to play the game, Herr Hauptmann?"

Hobbs could feel the man's confusion. Hauptmann feigned more laughter, hesitantly. "Ha," he said. "No—thank you, *Herr Inspektor.* No, I would not."

"Ah, well. To be expected, I suppose."

He turned to Hobbs. He was a wolfish-looking man, hollow-cheeked and hooded-eyed. His expression, in the faint blue moonlight, was somber. "I suppose we'll need to proceed without any more games," he said. "Eh, Herr Hobbs?"

Hobbs didn't answer. After another moment, Frick reached into his pocket. Hobbs watched, feeling dizzy, his heartbeat a series of fast, shallow fillips.

When Frick withdrew his hand, there was a single chalky tablet of white in the center of his palm.

"This poison," Frick said benevolently, "is fatal in three seconds. You are fortunate, Herr Hobbs, that I am feeling merciful tonight."

He kept holding the pill forward. Hobbs kept looking at it. At last he reached for it, and took it between thumb and forefinger. The tablet felt very light and insubstantial, as if it was nothing but a product of his imagination.

The men in the front seat stared straight ahead, seemingly oblivious.

"Go on," Frick urged. "It is preferable to the other option."

Hobbs thought that he could hear a wisp of music: distant, keening notes. A bagpipe. Was it "Danny Boy"? He thought that it was.

He almost smiled. That song brought him back, all right. Countless nights in countless pubs, surrounded by his mates and singing rousing choruses of "Danny Boy." Nothing to worry about except staying sober enough to lift the next pint of courage. Those had been good days, he thought.

In the next instant, the music was gone.

"Go on," Frick said again, gently. "Show some dignity."

Hobbs looked back at him, taking the man's measure. He tried to picture himself lurching across the seat, incapacitating the Gestapo agent, and then slipping out of the car—without the ones up front moving to stop him.

He couldn't picture it.

"*Herr Inspektor*," Hauptmann said. "Perhaps we should return the man to Number Eight. He may be able to offer—"

Frick silenced the man with a glance. Then he turned back to Hobbs. "We are waiting," he said.

Hobbs put the pill onto his tongue. At first, it was tasteless. Then, as it dissolved, it turned bitter.

He leaned back in his seat, closing his eyes. Soon, now, the pain would go away. He wondered if Eva had made it to the extraction site. It would be nice to think that she had. It would be nice to think that he had done something right, before he left this world, by giving her a way out of Germany—that he had done something to make up, at least in part, for all his previous wrongs.

His head was growing lighter. He thought that he could feel his consciousness leaving his body, rising through the roof of the car, untethered. It was a liberating feeling; and, mercifully, there was no pain.

Three seconds, he thought.

They passed.

He was still alive.

He opened his eyes.

Frick was smiling at him. "How do you feel?" he asked.

Hobbs said nothing.

"I seem to have made a mistake," Frick said. "It is only aspirin."

Then he threw back his head and laughed. The men up front also laughed—but apprehensively, without conviction.

"You should have seen your face," Frick said. "Hauptmann. Did you see his face?"

"I saw it," Hauptmann lied.

"Now *that* is a joke, Hauptmann. Perhaps you're right. Perhaps I am the one with a sense of humor, between the two of us."

"Perhaps you are," Hauptmann said, sounding distinctly nonplussed.

Frick's laughter dwindled. He sat for a few moments without moving, seemingly lost in thought. Then he said abruptly: "Get out of the car."

Hobbs sent his eyes from Frick to Hauptmann to the driver. Then he reached for the door. He stepped out, planting his left leg carefully, keeping the weight off his right. Frick came out the other side—a gun in his hand now, trained on Hobbs across the roof of the Mercedes.

He motioned Hobbs around the front of the car. Suddenly the headlights came on, glaring hot white. Hobbs could sense Frick coming up behind him, the Luger in his hand. The man's breathing was uneven, strained with excitement.

"On your knees," he commanded.

Hobbs looked at the ground. The ground looked damp. He didn't move. He wished he could hear "Danny Boy" again, one last time.

"On your knees," Frick said again.

Oldfield had taught Hobbs how to disarm a man standing behind him. But Hobbs, of course, had not been paying attention to the lesson. He remembered what he had been thinking about instead, with terrible clarity: a pretty young bird named Rose.

"Do not try my patience," Frick said. "I will not ask again."

What had Oldfield said? Something about dropping to the ground. Something about rolling, hooking the man's legs with his ankles. He could almost catch the memory. But his mind had been on Rose.

If only Frick was facing him, he thought then. He remembered that lesson clearly enough. It had been a grisly one, and had imprinted itself on his brain. *If you can goad the man into placing the gun against your chest,* Oldfield had said, *then you have him.*

He started to turn; but Frick brought the gun down across his skull, driving him to his knees. An instant later, cool metal touched his head an inch below his right ear. The Luger. He squeezed his eyes closed, bracing himself.

Then nothing.

Frick cursed softly.

"Hauptmann," he called.

Hobbs opened his eyes again, and chanced a glance over his shoulder. The stocky man was coming out the passenger side of the car and stepping forward, backlit by the glow from the headlights. Frick muttered something and handed him the Luger. Hauptmann gave the man his own gun: a Walther P38.

Hobbs gritted his teeth, and—surprising himself—found the wherewithal to rise again to his feet. When Frick turned and saw this, his face registered mild shock. And below that, if Hobbs wasn't mistaken, was a glint of admiration.

Frick placed the gun against his chest. "Turn around," he commanded. "There is no—"

Hobbs did it exactly the way Oldfield had shown him.

He slapped down at the Walther P38 with his right hand; the web between his thumb and forefinger fell neatly between the hammer and the firing pin. When Frick pulled the trigger, the metal hit the skin, pinching; but the gun did not discharge. He immediately twisted the barrel back toward Frick, trapping the man's finger inside the trigger guard. Then stepped away, jerking the gun down, rotating it in the same motion. The metal edges of the trigger guard did their work, just as Oldfield had said they would.

Frick's index finger was torn from his hand.

I'll be goddamned, Hobbs thought wildly. *It worked.*

He pulled the gun free, shook the severed finger loose. He was dimly conscious of it flying off into the forest, turning end over end. He slipped his own finger over the trigger, leveled his arm, and fired a single shot into Frick's head.

Frick tumbled backward. Hauptmann was staring, astonished—and then he was running, slipping away into the darkness. Hobbs fired once at the man's back. Missed.

He turned to the Mercedes and fired at the driver. The wind-shield starred but held. *Bulletproof*, he thought. *God damn it.*

He dropped to the ground.

Frick was looking at him. A bloody furrow had opened on one side of the man's head. His eyes rolled. Hobbs started to bring the gun around, to finish the job, when he heard the sound of the Mercedes' other door opening. He turned his head and saw a boot stepping onto the forest floor. He aimed and fired; the foot jerked, and the man cried out.

He reached for the fender, pulling himself up. His leg was producing sharp, regular bolts of pain. But the pain cleared his head; the pain kept him alert.

The man he had shot in the foot was sitting on the forest floor, grappling after a gun that had fallen a few feet away. Hobbs stepped around the door and shot the man in the stomach.

Then turned back to Frick. Frick had dragged himself out of the pool of light. Hobbs saw one foot, skittering away through the brush. Only grazed, he thought.

And where was Hauptmann? Somewhere in the forest. But he had given Frick his gun, and taken the Luger. And the Luger had jammed.

The man he had gut-shot was moaning. Hobbs turned back to him and fired again, painting the side of the sedan with a grisly mixture of blood, tissue, and teeth.

The smell of cordite reached his nostrils, mixed with the stomach-turning stench of fresh blood. He bent over, dry-heaving.

Then he swallowed, straightened, and looked around. Frick had vanished, pulling himself away through the leaves like a snake. Hauptmann was nowhere to be seen. *I'll be goddamned*, he thought again. *It worked.*

He shoved the corpse away from the door and slipped behind the wheel of the Mercedes. The keys were in the ignition. He reached for them, started the engine, and pulled the door closed. He jammed his foot down on the gas and wheeled the car around, spewing dirt and leaves from the tires in two graceful arcs, snapping the other door shut in the process.

A moment later, he had found the road that was not a road. He glanced into the rearview mirror, looking for Frick or Hauptmann; but there was no sign of them.

His head was pounding. But he had done it. He had escaped. And he even had a car—a blessed car.

Eva, he thought.

There was still time.

He opened up the engine and the Mercedes jounced over the rough ground, gaining speed.

Chapter Fourteen

GOTHMUND

Eva knew—in a sinking, helpless way that did her no good whatsoever—that it was only a dream.

In the dream, the dogs were getting louder. She looked to her left, through the open window of the Volkswagen, and then to her right. The signs of the crossroads had been taken down. *In case of invasion*, she thought; *to confuse the enemy*. But as a result she didn't know which way to turn. And the dogs were growing ever louder.

She turned right.

Trees flashed past in a blur. She applied another cautious ounce of pressure to the gas. Every bump in the road was magnified, shaking the chassis like a miniature earthquake. A disturbing image appeared in her mind's eye: the Hindenburg going down in a roiling ball of flame. She took her foot from the gas and touched the brake.

Nothing happened.

She pumped the brake again; but the car didn't slow. Now the dog's hoarse barks were being left behind, and there was something in the road ahead. A fallen tree. She clutched the wheel tighter.

In the last instant before collision, she screamed.

When she came to, the dogs were close again.

She dragged herself to her feet. A frozen lake was spread before her, mirror-bright. She turned to look up the bank, at a great tangle of roots, and then down, at a deadfall that rose above her chest. Passage in either direction would be impossible. But the frozen lake presented its own problems—for she knew with sickening surety that the ice was thin, wafer-thin, deadly thin.

One dog howled: a long, lowing sound that sent shivers up her spine.

She stepped onto the ice.

For a few paces, she thought she would be all right. She fixed her eyes on the far bank, moving out across the lake under a sky the color of candle wax mixed with ash. After another few moments, she had made the halfway point. Too far to go back.

The first creak of the ice was slow, growling, in so low a register that it was almost inaudible.

Then the cracks were spreading out from her feet in a delicate web. The ice around her separated into floes, with frigid water pooling up between the cracks. The floe on which she stood was bobbing, crackling, buckling.

Eva held her breath; then the ice beneath her feet splintered apart and she plunged into the freezing lake.

"Kinder, Kirche, Küche," her mother said.

She was looking at Eva with kind, reproachful eyes—mothering eyes; smothering eyes. There was a cup of steaming hot tea in her hands, and she held it forward, tipping it to Eva's lips. Then she leaned back and said it again, this time in English:

"Children, church, kitchen. That's where a woman belongs, Eva. That's all she need concern herself with."

Eva didn't argue. She had taken ill from her fall in the lake; she was shivering, soaked in cold sweat. But at least she had left the dogs behind. At least she was safe here at home, in her childhood room, in her childhood bed.

"You shouldn't have forgotten that," her mother said. "I hope you've learned your lesson. No more of this business, Eva. It doesn't suit you. Promise me."

"I promise," Eva said.

Now her mother was Gretl, the girl with whom she worked at the Rundfunk.

"Besides," Gretl said. "He's very good-looking."

Eva was baffled. Gretl read it on her face and nodded toward the door. Hobbs was there, leaning jauntily in the doorway, smiling his lopsided smile.

"Why don't you marry him, Eva? For goodness sake, look how much he loves you. Look how much he's risked to warn you."

195

"He's not . . . steady."

"Nobody's perfect," Gretl said.

She looked at Hobbs again. He shrugged, seemingly amused.

"Maybe," she allowed.

"Here. Take your medicine."

She looked back at Gretl. Now Gretl had become Klinger. Klinger was reaching forward with a hand full of pills. But there was something wrong with that hand, Eva saw. There were too many fingers on it.

She closed her mouth, shook her head.

"*Liebling*," Klinger said. "It's best for you."

His hand moved toward her face again. There were thirteen fingers on that hand. She turned her face away, suddenly awash in revulsion.

"Take your medicine, Eva."

The fingers were intruding into her mouth. Peeling aside her lips, trying to penetrate the teeth. "Swallow it," Klinger said.

She shook her head again.

"Don't be a fool. Swallow it."

"Mm-mm."

"God damn it," he said. "*You take your medicine when I tell you to!*"

His other hand came up. There was a knife in it, wickedly sharp: a Hitler Youth dagger. She caught a flash of the legend emblazoned on the side. *Blut und Ehre.* Blood and honor.

Before she could move, the dagger had slid into her chest, sharp and smooth. Her mouth yawned open in a silent scream. The thirteen fingers slipped inside. She could feel them on her tongue, tickling like spider's legs. The pills dribbled down her throat.

"Now swallow," Klinger said.

She woke with a muffled gasp.

.   .   .

Outside, the wind soughed quietly through the trees. Branches pattered softly against the window. She sat motionless for a moment, letting the dream fade from her system.

A nightmare, she thought.

She was not cut out for this. Whatever potential Hobbs had thought he had seen in her, in that long-ago dream that had once been her life, was not there.

But soon enough it would be over. This was her last night in Gothmund. Her last night in Germany.

From the next room came the sound of Brandt's labored snoring. She considered sneaking out past him, for a breath of fresh air. But no; there were the neighbors. Even in the middle of the night, it would not be safe. For the neighbors already suspected her. To give them any more fodder for their suspicions would be unwise.

Tomorrow she would be on her way. Then all of their suspicions wouldn't matter.

She got out of bed and then stood hugging herself, with nowhere to go.

She had made it. She was safe. She had even managed to complete her mission. *Schlieffen*. It meant something. *They will know*.

And she had done it by herself—without Hobbs.

Hobbs.

She smiled to herself, faintly.

That ridiculous false mustache. Just an oversized schoolboy, she thought, playing at being an adult. But then, that was Hobbs all over.

She caught herself. That was how he got you, of course. That

197

immature charm. But he was worthless, when it came down to the real things in life. He was skilled as a drinking companion, gifted as a card player, and passable as a lover—just barely passable— but as a husband, or even a friend? He could not be trusted.

But then there was the letter. *I hope you can find it in your heart to forgive me.* As if he still loved her. As if he wanted another chance.

Foolishness, she thought.

She sat on the edge of the bed, and began to twist a lock of hair around her index finger.

First of all, it wasn't true. It was, doubtless, just another manipulation. Hobbs and his higher-ups at Whitehall wanted results, and they knew that Eva was likely no longer in thrall to them—after so many years, after so many miles—and so they had decided to manipulate her once again.

She could picture Hobbs and Cecil Oldfield sitting in the elder man's office at Leconfield House and drafting the letter, every word a calculation. *If she feels she's been hung out to dry, what's the best way to make her snap to?* By dangling Hobbs one more time, of course. The old carrot on the stick, to draw the horse and the cart. It had worked once; perhaps it would work again.

But they knew she was no fool. And so they had honed their strategy. *I hope you can find it in your heart to forgive me.*

Because she was the most important thing to Hobbs, in this fictional construct. That would be the way to get the results they wanted. Simply cracking the whip one more time would not spur this particular horse again. No; it was the carrot on the stick.

And even if there *was* a grain of truth in it . . .

But there wasn't.

But even if there *was*, it didn't change a thing.

Hobbs begging forgiveness. Her first reaction had been that she never would have thought she'd see the day. But now her mind, energized by several days' rest, saw the larger context. Suppose Hobbs *had* been begging forgiveness. Suppose he *did* think he had let something precious slip away, when he had let her go. It still didn't change a thing.

It was easy, of course, to misbehave and then apologize. The difficult thing was to take the responsibility, to do the correct thing, the first time out. Hobbs apologizing should not have surprised her. Apologies were what weak men gave, instead of results.

And Hobbs was a weak man. A charming one, from time to time. In his element, when the light was right. But a weak one. She was better off without him.

Outside, the wind rose; she shivered. She got back into bed, drawing the blankets up to her chin.

Tomorrow. England.

Home, she supposed. As close to home as she had.

Once she passed on what Klinger had told her, Germany would be closed to her. But Nazi Germany was not her home anyway. The Germany that she had cared for was gone, a thing of the past, a relic that existed only in memory and the fisherman's paintings.

But what about her family? She had brothers. Had they joined up? By passing on Klinger's secrets, would she be putting them in danger?

There was no use in worrying about it. Her choices had been made long before. It was too late to change her mind now.

She listened to the old man's snoring, and wondered. Yes, it was too late to change her mind now.

And it was almost over.

She wanted nothing more than to have it over.

WISMAR

$\mathcal{H}$auptmann conferred with the *Regierungsrat*, then came to the corner of the police station where Frick sat holding the ice wrapped in cloth pressed to his temple.

"He has placed the call," Hauptmann reported. "Another car will be here in a matter of minutes."

Frick nodded, and took the cloth away from his head. The cloth was stained with dark blood. He looked at it for a moment, clinically, then pressed it back again.

"But he is concerned," Hauptmann said. "He believes you require medical attention, *Herr Inspektor.* And I must say that I agree with him. Leave the man to me."

Frick scowled. "Out of the question."

"But you are unwell. Your head; and your hand—"

"I am fine."

"Herr Inspektor—"

"Fine," Frick repeated. "The Mercedes had very little petrol. The Engländer will soon be on foot again. In his current condition, he is nearly helpless. And so we will have him. Then, and only then, I will receive whatever medical attention I may require."

"*Herr Inspektor,*" Hauptmann said. "Be reasonable."

Frick started to growl a response . . .

. . . and then stopped.

When he shot the girl, her wide eyes grew even wider.

She tumbled back into the ditch. But she wasn't dead yet. He knew that even before he had stepped to the edge to check on her.

She was lying amidst a jumble of wan, dirty limbs—her family's limbs. The bullet had taken her in the side of the throat. The wound was ragged, and whistling. Her eyes pinned him. Burned into him. *Eighteen*, he thought.

He raised the gun and fired again.

Then he looked over his shoulder, hoping nobody had noticed. It was a waste of ammunition. Two bullets on one Jew. If his aim had been true the first time . . .

Nobody seemed to have noticed. The nearest member of his *Einsatzgruppen* squad stood a dozen yards away, looking at the town on the horizon. The town was burning. Black smoke roiled up into the sky. The air smelled like the air of an abattoir.

Frick turned from the ditch. He felt a pang of guilt. Two bullets. But nobody had noticed. It would be all right. Nobody would ever know that he had wasted two bullets in executing the beautiful Jewish girl.

". . . headache?" Hauptmann was saying.

Frick saw that he was offering a small bottle. SS *Sanitäts* aspirin. He shook his head, then immediately regretted it.

"No. No need."

Hauptmann returned the aspirin to his pocket.

"At least let me find a doctor, to suture up your hand. We have hours of daylight left for tracking. The team from Berlin will not arrive for some minutes yet."

Frick considered, then nodded reluctantly. "Find the doctor."

He watched as Hauptmann turned and yelled an order to the *Regierungsrat*. The man liked giving orders, Frick thought. So many petty dictators in the world. But Hauptmann would not be allowed to usurp this operation. The Engländer was his quarry, and his alone. No matter if the bullet had grazed his head . . . no matter if his finger was gone . . .

His finger was gone.

The man had crippled him.

Nobody else would be allowed to take charge of the operation.

Hauptmann's voice was rising. "*Schnell*," he cried. "*Schnell*—"

His mother set the loaf of fresh-baked bread on the table. The smell of it gave Frick a feeling of peace—of being home, safe, and protected. A marvelous feeling.

Then she was setting the bread down once again; and then yet again. Time had ceased to move forward. There was no progression—only a pleasing constancy, an eternal repetition. The fresh bread, the thread of faraway music; sense-memories and that delicious feeling of *being back home*.

An Advent wreath hung from the ceiling, with four white candles guttering in a soft breeze. On the wall behind his head was the Advent calendar his father had made for him. Small paper windows dotted the calendar. Each morning until Christmas he would open one window and behind it find a treat: a chocolate, a ball, a candle. Was there any greater pleasure in life than the pleasure of counting down the days to Christmas on an Advent calendar? Was there any greater gift a man could receive than to relive that feeling over and over again?

Eighteen, the girl had said.

But that was only a dream. The reality was this: his mother forever setting down the bread, the four candles forever flickering . . .

.　.　.

The doctor was talking with Hauptmann.

Then he turned and came back to Frick. *"Herr Kriminal Inspektor,"* he said. "How do you feel?"

Frick only shrugged.

The doctor was a fat little man, shaped and colored like a plum. *A glutton*, Frick thought. He began to talk very quickly, using medical terms that Frick couldn't quite understand. A gluttonous fool, and yet another petty dictator. Why was the world filled with men such as this? Why had they not yet been swept aside?

". . . the bullet," the doctor was saying. "You are fortunate, in that regard. But I would hardly . . ."

Perhaps the man's words would have made sense, Frick thought, if only they hadn't been so busy. Yet they *were* busy—in constant motion, the precise opposite of the sense-memory about his mother. The consonants and vowels fought each other on their way out of the man's mouth, jockeying for position. His tongue and palate were too fast, too precise. Or was the problem in Frick's mind instead? He was seeing too much.

". . . program of rest," the doctor was saying now. "Fresh air and relaxation. Perhaps a sanitarium. I might be able to provide a—"

Frick stood, pushing the man aside. He had no time for this. He took a few steps into the center of the room and then came to a stop, lost.

Hauptmann approached him. "Do you see, *Herr Inspektor?* You are unwell. You must cede control of the operation—"

Frick looked at the man. The stocky little worm. Dead skin

cells sloughing off his body. Hauptmann was half-dead already, and didn't even realize it.

"You have a mother," Frick said. "Don't you?"

Hauptmann paused.

"Even a worm such as you has a mother," Frick said. "How would she like it, I wonder, in Moabit Prison? I have reason to suspect she has been producing newspapers, you see. Bolshevik propaganda. With one sweep of a pen . . ."

The color had drained from Hauptmann's face.

"My apologies," he said. "I can see that I was mistaken, Herr Frick. You are well after all."

"Address me by my proper title," Frick snapped.

"*Herr Kriminal Inspektor.* My apologies."

"Where is the car from Berlin?"

"Arriving momentarily, *Herr Kriminal Inspektor.*"

Frick nodded. "Assemble the men."

He should have accepted the aspirin, he thought as Frick skulked away. He had lost his own vial, somewhere in the woods.

And he had the beginning of a very bad headache.

LÜBECK

The Mercedes coughed, considered, and then died.

Hobbs looked at the petrol gauge for a moment. He reached out and tapped it. The needle stayed flat.

Then he grinned a black grin. Nothing could ever be easy.

He pushed open the door, limped to the boot of the Mercedes, and lifted it, thinking there might be something inside that he could use as a cane. He was not far from his destination. Just how close, he couldn't know. But too close to give up now.

The first thing he saw was a petrol can.

His grin returned. He grabbed the can, and knew immediately from the weight that it was empty. He shook the container and was rewarded only by an empty rattle. He flung it aside and bent down again.

A spare tire and a jack. He dug past them, his nose wrinkling at the fusty air of the trunk. A few oily rags and a pamphlet announcing a Strength Through Joy demonstration. He tossed it back. A moment later, he had found his satchel. When they had taken him, outside Wismar, they had also taken his things. Thrown them in the boot. But where was the rifle?

He leaned farther forward, searching. There it was—in the back of the trunk, having slid into a cranny behind the tire. He worked it free.

Before setting off, he opened the satchel and found his pack of Player's. Two cigarettes remained. And his book of matches, tucked inside. He shook a cigarette free and put it between his lips.

He lit it, then looked off over the land.

He had lost track of the days. Perhaps he had already missed the extraction. Perhaps Eva was already on her way back to England, and there would be nothing waiting for him even if he did manage to reach Gothmund.

But he wouldn't find out standing here, now, would he?

He gave himself five minutes—enough time to finish the cigarette, and to get used to the idea that there was more walking ahead.

His leg didn't like the idea. But his leg was outvoted.

He tossed the cigarette aside, planted the rifle, and took a first dogged step.

Chapter Fifteen

A small drama was playing out on the street before Number 8 Prinz Albrecht Strasse.

After watching for a few seconds, Frick turned. For some reason, the scene had unsettled him. He stood for a moment, trying to figure out why that should be. Because it reminded him of something he had forgotten. Something involving prisoners. But what?

"*Herr Kriminal Inspektor*," someone was saying.

Frick ignored the voice. He turned back to the window, to watch the denouement of the drama. Two wild dogs were fighting in the street. As he watched, one gained the upper hand; its jaws clamped down on the throat of the other. They rolled in a tangle of fur and switching tails. Blood sprayed. Then Gestapo agents were running forward, yelling and cursing. Four guns sounded at once. Both dogs rolled over, dead.

Except it wasn't the street outside Number 8 Prinz Albrecht Strasse.

It was the rolling hills outside Lübeck; night was just beginning to fall. And the dogs . . .

. . . the dogs were real.

"Fucking mutt," Hauptmann said, from somewhere very close by. "He killed Boche."

Around them, the division of Waffen SS, having gunned down the fighting dogs, milled aimlessly in the cool twilight. The abandoned Mercedes sat like an oversized dead snail. Two SS men stood by it, the embers of their cigarettes glowing intermittently.

"This is a setback," Hauptmann said seriously. "Boche is the only decent tracker we've got out here."

Frick said nothing. His headache was very bad—and still growing worse.

"What's the situation?" he asked tersely.

Hauptmann gave him an odd look.

"Nothing has changed," Hauptmann said then. "He must have continued on foot. But without Boche, I'm not certain we can track him. None of these other bitches are worth a thing."

The other bitches, Frick thought. At first he didn't know what Hauptmann meant by that. Then he looked around and saw a half-dozen dogs led by SS agents. He jerked his chin up and down, to show that he had understood.

"We are awaiting your order, *Herr Kriminal Inspektor*."

With a gargantuan act of will, Frick managed to focus.

"We will split into two groups," he said. "The man is badly wounded. We should catch up to him easily before dawn."

Hauptmann seemed satisfied with that. He turned and went to relay the orders. As he watched the man walk away, Frick's vision rippled. His headache swelled; twin stilettos slid into his temples. He nearly collapsed to his knees from the pain.

Dear God in Heaven, he thought. *Help me.*

Hauptmann was back—and looking at him strangely again. "The men are talking," he said in a low voice.

Frick found the agony in his head, isolated it, and did his best to dismiss it. "Talking," he repeated.

"They're nervous, *Herr Kriminal Inspektor.* The rifle is missing from the trunk; the man must have recovered it. And he is an excellent shot—remember Wismar."

Frick could hardly remember what they were talking about. *Wismar?* he thought.

Hauptmann took a step closer, and added in a voice barely above a whisper, "Also, they are doubting you, *Herr Kriminal Inspektor.*"

"Doubting me," Frick said.

"You seem . . . unwell. The doctor—"

"I will not brook insubordination," Frick said.

"No, of course not, *Herr Kriminal Inspektor.*"

"Impress that upon them, Herr Hauptmann."

Frick turned away as Hauptmann moved off, and looked over the dark swelling land. Hobbs was out there. Wounded. Not far away. He would have his man soon enough.

But there was a shape in the edge of his vision—a black something. As soon as he noticed it, he caught a sense of wings unfolding. Flapping lazily.

"*Achtung!*" Hauptmann yelled, and the men gave him their attention.

They were moving over black land.

Frick had his gun in his hand—another Luger, requisitioned from the *Regierungsrat.* Beside him were three other men, also with guns in their hands. One of the men was Hauptmann. Another held a leash; a German shepherd sniffed busily at the damp ground.

"He's got something," the man holding the leash said.

They all gathered around as the dog buried its muzzle in the earth. What did the dog have? Frick could not separate one thing from another. Then the dog looked up, whining. "This way," the man said, and they were off again.

The land was swampy. Countless small lakes, most no larger than ponds, dotted the landscape. The water glistened under the light of the rising moon. Not far away, a cluster of black trees poked into the sky. The dog led them in that direction; they followed at a trot.

"Here!" a man cried.

They were entering the trees. Frick's nostrils were suddenly filled with the rich smell of nature: pine and fir, sharp and overwhelming. Too much. He could not stand it any longer. He raised a hand to his head.

The black bird lurking in the edge of his vision flapped its wings again, slowly.

"*Herr Kriminal Inspektor . . .*"

His head was throbbing. Behind his eyes, he realized. That was where the problem was. And he would need to . . .

"*Herr Kriminal Inspektor . . .*"

. . .

"*Down*," Hauptmann hissed.

Frick blinked dumbly.

"*Down*," Hauptmann hissed again. Then a rifle cracked. Frick threw himself down.

The moon overhead, peeking through the waving branches of the trees. A face in the moon, smiling down. The soft wet ground below. The men around him, lying flat, staring into the night. He brought himself back to reality, concentrating on these things, sifting out the strongest impressions.

"What now?" Hauptmann asked.

Frick blinked again. The rifle cracked for a second time. The bullet whispered harmlessly through the leaves above him, stirring currents of air.

"I'll get behind him," one of the men announced, his voice thunderous, deafening.

He rose into a crouch. The rifle popped and he spilled backward with a truncated curse.

"Damn him," Hauptmann breathed. "He's a devil with that gun."

The man who was not Hauptmann elbowed forward in the muck. He had the German shepherd, Frick saw, still on the leash.

"Let the dog at him," Frick said.

"Are you insane? He's in the branches."

Another bullet pounded into the earth, spattering them with mud.

"We've got to move," Hauptmann said desperately. "Retreat. Find reinforcements."

"*Herr Kriminal Inspektor?*" the other man said.

211

"Forget him," Hauptmann said. "He's lost his mind."

A moment later, the two men were moving off, back in the direction of the moonlit lakes. Frick rolled onto his back and watched them go. *Traitors*, he thought. *Cowards*.

He rolled onto his stomach again. His head was throbbing horribly. There was an invader in there, behind his eyes. He would need to take action, he thought, to repel the invader. He would—

He saw Hobbs. His quarry.

Halfway up a slender tree; raising the rifle to his eye, taking aim.

Frick climbed forward, took shelter behind a wide trunk, and clumsily, with his left hand, checked the load in his Luger.

Hobbs saw the man making for the tree. There would just be time to make the shot—but when he squeezed the trigger, the hammer clicked sharply.

He reached to his belt for the last magazine, withdrew it, and then watched as it tumbled from his fingers, glanced off a branch, and struck the ground.

He stared in disbelief. He had dropped the last magazine. He could see it down there, half-buried in a pile of leaves. But the idea of scaling down the tree to retrieve it—in his current condition, with an armed man waiting to shoot him—was laughable.

He lowered the barrel of the Enfield, then brought one hand to his mouth and nibbled on the cuticle.

That was it, then.

After a few moments, he resettled himself on the branch, distributing his weight so that as little as possible rested on his ruined leg. The lone remaining man was still sheltered behind the tree. In a few moments, he would doubtless find the courage to make another try. And Hobbs would be stranded here, under the bright moonlight, like a target in a shooting gallery.

Somehow the thought was not as unsettling as it might have been. Death was coming for him—yet he had the oddly comforting feeling that he had been here before. He and Death had once known each other. Before he had ever been born, perhaps. Now they would find a chance to become reacquainted. What could be more natural? When a man's time came, his time came.

He took the last zigzagging cigarette from the pack, stuck it into his mouth, and lit it. Then he leaned back against the trunk, looking up through the leaves at the smiling moon. He drew deeply on the cigarette, savoring it. The tobacco was stale and half-rotten, but still soothing.

A night breeze ruffled his hair. He looked up at the stars; his head felt pleasantly light. What was taking the man so long? He was helpless, stranded up in this tree. He was ready to meet Death again—to put an end to all the struggle. *"He that dies pays all debts."* What was that from? Ah, well.

His thoughts turned to Eva. Had she made it to Gothmund? His intuition was that she had. Eva would make it back to England. It was his time, but not yet hers. And that seemed natural.

Natural—but not right. For there was some other intuition about Eva, scraping at the edges of his mind. *The bait and switch*, he thought. She was the bait. And the switch was . . .

The thought was interrupted by a soft sound. He strained, listening. Just the wind?

No.

He crinkled his eyes in disbelief.

The man behind the tree was weeping.

There was something in Frick's head. Something very wrong. It burned.

He clawed at the skin on his face, trying to peel it back, to gain access to the rot that had worked its way into his brain. But the skin wouldn't come. He sniffed, wiped a hand across his nose, and then withdrew his dagger from its sheath.

He began to pray in murmurs, long-forgotten Christian prayers that somehow found their way to his tongue without passing through his brain. At the same time, he pressed the edge of the blade against his cheek and then drew it down. The skin peeled off in a thin, curling ribbon. His blood welled, suppurated. Diseased blood. Still burning. He needed to get it out of himself. Immediately.

The knife moved down, then up again, then down again.

His lips drew back from his teeth. He kept working, whittling away at himself.

Black things. Fell things. They were inside him; they were a part of him.

The smell of fresh bread, heady and ripe.

Hobbs dropped onto the ground, keeping the scream clenched behind his teeth.

For an instant, he balanced like a stork. Then he planted the barrel of the Enfield and began to shuffle forward. If he tried for the magazine, he would lose his balance. Better to do it himself, by hand, while there was still a chance that the man behind the tree was distracted.

The man continued to weep. Between the tears, he was muttering to himself. Then even the muttering was quieted, as if something had interfered with the man's tongue. Before rounding the tree, Hobbs tried to figure how he would strike a blow without falling over. He would have one chance to swing the rifle; then he would come tumbling down. But he would make the blow count.

He rounded the tree.

And froze, astounded.

In his last moment, Frick looked up and saw the Engländer looking down at him, his mouth hanging open in shock.

Their eyes met, and something passed between them.

Then the winged creature took slow, clumsy flight. Frick fell onto one side. The knife tumbled from his lifeless fingers. His senses were shutting down—*Praise God*, he thought; *merciful to the end*.

A gossamer cloud passed in front of the moon, and somewhere in the distance a night bird trilled with eerie beauty.

Chapter Sixteen

GOTHMUND

Don't forget," Brandt said. "Give Noyce my message."

Eva nodded remotely, then looked around, found a fallen tree, and sat down on it with her case in her lap.

Brandt hovered for a few seconds, wondering whether or not he should wish her luck. He decided that it was unnecessary. They both wanted nothing more than to be rid of each other. So of course he wished her luck; it went without being said. He turned away without another word, and began to pick his way back toward town under a sky the color of bruises.

It wasn't his problem if the woman wanted to sit out in the woods, alone. It was her own fault for not knowing the precise time of the extraction. He certainly didn't need to wait here with her. Who knew when—or even if—the plane would arrive?

He was finished. His duties were discharged.

As he was essaying a rough spot in the path, he felt a sudden and guilty surge of conscience. Look at him: so eager to disassociate himself. He was a coward, in his heart. He should wait with the girl to make sure she was met—out of chivalry, if for no better reason. But instead he was moving away. Instructing her to tell Noyce he was finished. Taking the easy way out.

But he had not gotten into this for the purpose of doing what was right. He had become involved only from necessity, he reminded himself, in order to keep his secret. Perhaps he didn't agree with the politics of the Nazis. It would have been difficult for any man in his position to agree with those tremendously intolerant politics. Perhaps he doubted the path along which Hitler was leading his people. But many others felt the same. And they had done even less than Brandt had done. They had simply sat back, watching and waiting to see what the outcome would be—or joined in, anticipating rich rewards.

Politics were only politics. His life, in comparison, was his life. Who would expect a man to extend himself, once he had guaranteed his personal security, for the sake of politics?

Nobody, was the answer. Nobody would expect that, except an idealistic fool.

But if the girl failed to make it back to England, he thought, then perhaps Noyce would decide that he had failed to hold up his end of the bargain. Perhaps he would somehow contrive a method of letting the villagers know about Brandt's predilections. He thought of his neighbors. The way they looked at him now was bad enough. The way they would look at him if they knew . . .

That would be a fate worse than death. The shame would be too much to bear.

But she would make it back, he thought.

In any case, he could hardly wave a magic wand and make the airplane appear. Either it did or it didn't. It was beyond his control.

He reached the Fischerweg and closed the distance to his house, moving deliberately, suddenly feeling very old.

He went back to his painting. But the desire to paint was gone. He just stood, looking out at the windswept harbor, thinking.

Not his problem. He was finished.

Nobody could blame a man for not extending himself beyond the point of personal interest. Those who did would be hypocrites.

And who was to say, in any case, what was right and what was wrong? It was possible that by serving the British, Brandt had contributed to an evil even greater than that of the Nazis. There were very few absolute truths in the world, he thought. Hitler had done good things for Germany. If Brandt *was* to return to the field, to make certain that the plane arrived to meet the woman, he would be doing it for selfish reasons. To guarantee his own personal privacy. Not for any larger reason than that; and there was no point in pretending otherwise.

The Nazis had been good for Germany, he thought again. They had brought his people from the brink of disaster to their current position, poised to conquer the planet.

And if they'd given up a few things in the process . . .

. . . such as free imperial city status, for the town of Lübeck; such as a man's right to be whatever that man wanted to be, in a country where, during recent years, such men had enjoyed greater freedom of expression than in any other quarter of the world . . .

. . . well, then it had been worth the sacrifice.

He stared at the painting. This ancient German town. He could feel his inspiration deserting him. He had painted it too many times before. He had nothing else to add.

Then a new painting occurred to him: the fabulous Unter den Linden of Berlin, which he had seen as a young man. A gorgeous avenue, wide and grand, with spectacular lime trees lining the edges like verdant soldiers standing at attention.

He removed the canvas from the easel, replaced it with a blank one, and debated how to begin.

Even before he'd applied the first stroke, he lost the will to proceed. For the Unter den Linden, of course, had been ruined by the Nazis. Hitler had cut down the lime trees to make space for his endless military processions. Now the pride of Berlin—a street called Under the Lime Trees—featured no lime trees.

A travesty, he thought.

He stood for some unknowable length of time, the brush held loosely in one hand, staring at nothing. The quality of the light changed, thinning, turning gold.

Then, with a muttered curse, he set down the brush and turned back to the door.

LAKE WANNSEE

𝕳agen sat still for a moment after hanging up the telephone.

Then, suddenly, he swept the phone off his desk in a fit of pique and a riot of fluttering papers.

Hobbs, he thought.

It would be a mistake to take it personally. It would be a mistake to confuse the professional with the personal.

And yet that was precisely what he was doing.

According to the report he had just received over the telephone, the man had murdered his agent with a savagery that struck Hagen as diabolically intentional. Frick had been butchered like a animal. As if Hobbs had made sadistic sport of the killing, he thought bitterly, knowing full well that an account would be delivered back to Hagen.

It was a message of some kind, from Hobbs to him. A final twist of the knife, to drive home just how severely Hagen had underestimated the man. It almost seemed as if Hobbs had known the investment that Hagen had made in Frick, as if he had been determined to deny Hagen the satisfaction of a worthy successor . . .

. . . no; he was reading too much into it. He forced himself to calm down.

The situation was not beyond repair.

In fact the situation—if Hagen was able to get far enough outside his personal interests to look at it rationally—could hardly have been better. The Bernhardt woman was at Gothmund, under observation by Himmler's agents. The OKW clerk Klinger had delivered the false intelligence to her, and now she would pass it on to the British. The entire deception had gone flawlessly, from beginning to end.

221

Except for Hobbs. Hobbs had proven far more capable than Hagen had assumed.

What was driving the man?

Hagen saw two possibilities. The first struck him as almost droll. Perhaps Hobbs was displaying such unexpected resourcefulness because he fancied the Bernhardt girl more than anyone had understood. Hagen had seen photographs of the two together, entering the Right Club in London years before—but he had also seen photographs of Hobbs with many other young women taken during those years. He had imagined that the Bernhardt girl was just another distraction to the man, with no special importance. But perhaps he had imagined wrong. He would never completely understand the lengths to which some men would go for certain women. Did they not realize that the world was overflowing with women, each much the same as the next?

If that were the case, there was no need for special concern. Even if Hobbs did manage to reach Gothmund, he would do everything in his power to make sure the woman boarded the plane safely. And so he would be unwittingly playing, yet again, directly into Hagen's hands.

But the second possibility was disturbing. Perhaps Hobbs had somehow figured out the truth behind the operation. This seemed unlikely, almost to the point of impossibility. Yet if it were true, it could have serious repercussions. For if Hobbs managed to reach the woman and deliver a warning before she had safely boarded the British plane sent to evacuate her, then the operation might still be compromised.

How could Hobbs have figured it out?

He could not have. Even those with far more clues than Hobbs—Admiral Canaris and SD Chief Heydrich among them—had not figured it out. Only three men in all of Germany knew the details of the operation. That was how Hitler had wanted it, of course. In the upper echelons of the Nazi party, every man looked out for himself. Had the details fallen into the wrong hands, self-interest might have motivated any number of men to interfere with the completion of the operation.

And so participants had been limited to three: Hitler, Reichsleiter Himmler, and Hagen himself.

The idea had come from Hitler. When an airplane carrying the plans for the offensive against the West had gone down at Mechelen-sur-Meuse, the past January, the Luftwaffe officer on board had failed to burn the documents before they had fallen into the hands of the Belgian police. A lesser man than Hitler would have taken this development as a serious hindrance; but Hitler had managed to turn the situation to his benefit. From the debris of one operation, he had planted the seeds of another. He had personally devised the maneuver that had recently been put into effect, and as a result the Nazis' chances of conquering the land to the west were far greater than ever before.

Without Hitler's hubris, the plan would never have been concocted. But without Hagen's own inspired contributions, it never would have played out so well. For when Hitler had come to Himmler, looking for a method to deliver his false secrets, Himmler had come to Hagen—and Hagen had suggested the use of the Bernhardt woman.

He already had known, of course, Hobbs' true purpose in coming to Germany. The loss of the man Teichmann had caused anxiety throughout all of the Nazi intelligence organizations. It was only a matter of time before the British would take action to check the man's information. In preparation for this event, the remaining members of the MI6 network had been placed under surveillance. As soon as the man Waldoff had rendezvoused in the park with the Bernhardt woman, Hagen had realized—as he already had suspected—that there was another network within Germany, a network still unknown to them. The Bernhardt woman was a part of this network, and Hobbs' purpose in coming to Germany had been to make contact with her. And so Hagen had been able to give Hitler the perfect vessel for his deception.

Hobbs had been allowed to reach the woman, and the woman had been allowed to reach the OKW clerk Klinger. Yet the secrets told by the clerk had been misleading—for Hagen had reached Klinger first.

Now the Allies would expect a repeat of the Schlieffen strategy, which had nearly given the Germans such fine results during the Great War: a drive through the Low Countries and then Sedan, with the aim of capturing Paris. Their expectations would be validated by a feint to the north, and they would move in that direction to repel the anticipated attack. Then the Wehrmacht's surprise strike through the Ardennes would catch them completely off guard. Paris would be bypassed, the port territory captured. And the Allied troops would be cut off from supply lines, surrounded, doomed.

Yes, the deception had gone flawlessly. But if Hobbs had somehow managed to guess the truth, then he could not be allowed to reach the Bernhardt woman with a possible warning.

From one pocket, Hagen removed a watch on a fine silver chain. He would go to Gothmund himself, this very evening. The woman was under surveillance by Himmler's agents—but they did not know how capable the Engländer had turned out to be.

Hagen would educate them on that development. And if in the process he found the chance to deal with Hobbs himself—to exact some measure of revenge for the loss of his prized agent Frick—that would just be a bonus.

He stood. Time was short; but he dallied for another minute before leaving the office. The sense of betrayal, of disappointment, filled him with rage. It would not do to let the rage take control. He had spent too much time in offices lately, and not enough time in the field. If he planned on involving himself in the operation personally, he would need to do so with a level head. So the rage must be controlled.

But his entire career, it sometimes seemed, had been a series of disappointments. Katarina; Frick; Hobbs. Why was it so? What had he done to deserve this?

His rage, he realized then, was mixed with something else: a sense of panic. If a man did his level best and events still careened out of control, then what did a man have? He was simply flotsam on the tide of fate.

He controlled his breathing. Steady; in and out.

After a few moments, he felt calmer. He pressed his lips into a thin line and then went to the closet to find his customized black uniform. His work clothes.

The uniform, he was pleased to discover, still fit.

THE BALTIC SEA

The unbroken plain of water gave way, on the distant horizon, to a dark shelf of land—the northern coast of Germany.

Deacon's body had been tingling with adrenaline ever since

he had taken off from Sweden in the late afternoon. Now, however, it was reaching a new level. This was no mere confetti
campaign, after all. This was something altogether different.
Moreover, it was a chance at long-awaited justice.

For most of the flight, Deacon had been thinking about justice. There was a pleasant irony to be found, he thought, in the
fact that it would come from this flight over churning black
water. Twenty-five years before, a similar flight, but moving
over a different body of water, had ended in the murder of his
parents. The zeppelin bombing raids of Kaiser Wilhelm, the
first major aerial bombardment in history, had ravaged his
family—and many other innocent Britishers—with indiscrimi-
nate carnage.

But his vengeance would be softer, subtler, more honorable.
The Germans, on that night in October 1915, had pummeled
their enemies with a clenched fist of fire. Now he would find retri-
bution with a glove of silk. He would peck them a stolen kiss in
the night, and at the same time would sweep their plans for world
domination right out from under their goose-stepping heels.

The Lysander felt good under his touch—responsive, but not
overeager. The plane had not originally been built with this purpose in mind. It had been built for observation, and the occasional "army cooperation": snagging messages with a dangling
hook, strafing ground targets with one of its twin Browning
machine guns. But now, thanks to a few simple modifications, it
was an entirely different beast. It could sneak into enemy territory, land on a field the size of a large postage stamp, and take off
again from rough terrain. A quick kiss in the night. But one that
would change the course of history.

Lofty thoughts. But then, he'd always had a flair for drama.

Besides, beneath the adrenaline was something else. A constant undertow of fear that threatened to sweep him away, to drag him under. If lofty thoughts kept that at bay, then so be it.

So be it, he thought.

He nudged the controls in his hands, and the sea beneath him turned to land.

GOTHMUND

Hagen found the men clustered in a group, their nerves crackling.

"Report," he said.

The Gestapo man who stepped forward had uneven eyes, a nose reddened from too much drink, and fingers stained brown from too much tobacco.

"The girl is sitting on the edge of the field. Just waiting, it seems. The fisherman left her alone several hours ago. Braun—spyglass."

The spyglass was handed to the Gestapo man, then to Hagen. He raised it to his eyes and immediately found the girl, sitting on a log, looking as if she were waiting for a bus.

He kept watching as the man talked on.

"We have two agents posted on the far side of the lake. Two others in the bushes along the western perimeter of the field. Two others along the eastern. And ourselves."

Hagen handed the spyglass back. "No sign of the Engländer?"

"None, *Herr Obersturmführer.*"

Hagen wondered how the man had chosen that rank for him.

He considered correcting him, then decided against it. If they believed he was Gestapo instead of SD, they would be more willing to take his orders without complaint.

"Is the fisherman still under observation?"

"No, *Herr Obersturmführer*. We needed the manpower here. Besides, he's done his work already."

"He should be arrested," Hagen said.

"When it's finished, *Herr Obersturmführer*, I'll see to it myself."

"The girl is not to be interfered with. She must believe that she has thrown off any pursuit. If Hobbs does appear, he must be apprehended silently."

"The men have their orders, sir. No gunfire."

"Let me have the glass again."

He trained the spyglass back on the Bernhardt girl. Such an ordinary-looking girl, he thought. Such a fragile shell, for such a vital operation. But that was the stroke of genius. No one would suspect that she had been part of a brilliant deception. She did not even suspect it herself.

It might even have been worth losing Frick, he thought then. *It might have been worth losing a dozen men, or a hundred, or a thousand, to get the girl safely onto that plane.*

There would be other pupils, other protégés. Besides, there had always been something slightly *off* about Frick, hadn't there? His eagerness to volunteer for duty on the front in Poland. His peculiar way of being in a room and not being there at the same time. And something in his eyes—something unnatural.

He handed the spyglass back again.

Hobbs would not make it, he thought. He may have found unexpected resources within himself, but a man was what a man was. And Hobbs, in Hagen's opinion, was not much of a man.

He looked up at the sky. The night was brilliantly clear, with the heavens sprawled in all their glory. The dark clouds were very high, so high that they seemed to brush against the stars themselves. He could not have wished for better weather. The operation would be a success.

There was nothing he liked better than a successful operation.

Soon now, he thought.

Soon.

Hobbs could live without the leg.

Exhibit A, he thought; the fact that he was still moving.

The leg was still attached to his body, but it was useless— beyond useless; an encumbrance. And yet he continued moving, leaning on the rifle in one hand and an improvised walking stick in the other. He was approaching the extraction site, and he had done it without the leg. So life would go on. He and Eva would return to England and live in the country, in a beautiful house, and life would go on. They would have many children. The children would bring him the things he needed without his having to stand. He would take up cribbage. And he would cheat.

But first, he would need to get on that plane with Eva.

He would manage it.

Behind him the town of Gothmund lay slumbering. He had circled it, deciding instead to head directly to the field. He didn't know what day it was, but it must have been late. And if he had guessed correctly, they would have had the fisherman under surveillance in any case. But if he had guessed correctly, they would also allow Eva to get aboard the plane. She would be allowed to reach the field. So the field it was.

The guess had been welling in his mind for the past few fever-
ish hours. It had come from nowhere, from his subconscious—
yet he knew, somehow, that it was correct. It explained the reason
Hagen left him under the poor oversight of Borg, the reason he
had been sent to Berlin after his months at Lake Wannsee instead
of being executed right then.

Eva was not the bait—the OKW clerk had been the bait. And
the switch was the intelligence he would give her, the strategy to
be followed by the Wehrmacht. Whatever the clerk had told Eva
would be exactly wrong. The Allies would expect the Nazis to follow one course of action. They would follow the opposite—and
Europe would be theirs.

If he could get aboard that plane, however, then he would
frustrate Hagen even at this late stage in the game. He would show
the man that he could not out-con a con man. If he could just get
on that plane . . .

He had left the satchel behind. The sole remaining magazine
for the Enfield was jammed into his belt, prodding into his hip
with each lurching step. There were five bullets in the magazine.
That would be five dead Nazis—for Hagen would doubtless have
Eva under close watch.

The fever was unfortunate. But he would manage.

The smell of standing water reached his nose. A moment
later, he saw the small lake. The surface was perfectly still, covered with a thin sheet of algae. Two silhouetted figures stood on
the near bank. They were evidence, he thought, that his guess had
been correct. Every move made by Eva was being watched, confirmed, and no doubt relayed back to Hagen.

Hobbs concealed himself behind a wide-reaching oak, then
peeked out warily.

The men were facing away from him, looking off at the field on the other side of the water.

After looking for a moment, he turned his eyes up to the tree. From the ground, he couldn't see the field clearly enough. There must have been other men posted around. If he simply walked out into the open, he might manage to kill one or two—but the remainder would gun him down like a dog. If he knew all of their positions, however, he could make every bullet count.

Five bullets. Would it be enough?

A low-hanging branch was within reach. But he felt dizzy again. If he tried to climb the tree, he might well catch the men's attention. Even worse, he might lose his grip and come crashing back down.

But perhaps he could climb the side of the oak facing away from the field. Perhaps he could do it quietly, and set himself up in the branches without being noticed. If only he could still feel his leg . . .

Nothing ventured, he thought, *nothing gained.*

He strapped the Enfield over his shoulder and reached for the low-hanging branch.

Eva was hungry.

Her stomach growled—loud enough to embarrass her, although there was nobody there to hear it. She thought of the meal she would have once she arrived back in England. The food in England was terrible. Just thinking about it made her appetite shrivel.

She looked out across the dark field, at the gentle motion of the grass in the wind, at the lake on the far end. The lake smelled of rich, ripe decay. She would not enjoy sitting here for very much longer. But who knew when the plane would arrive? She might have a day, or even two, to spend sitting on this log. If it came to that, perhaps she would go back to the fisherman's house after all. A meal, a bed.

She immediately changed her mind. The solitude was agreeable. She would rather sit here, hungry and cold but alone, than go back to the little house on the Fischerweg.

She pictured Hobbs at that moment: probably cuddled up with some German girl in a warm room, in a warm bed. Probably drunk on schnapps or whiskey. Had he tried to honor his rendezvous at the fisherman's house, and simply lost his resolve? It seemed likely. That was the Hobbs she knew—quick to accept a challenge, but slow to follow through. Perhaps something else had happened. Perhaps he'd truly been unable to make it to Gothmund. But she doubted it.

For a time, she distracted herself with a fantasy of what her new husband might look like. He would be British, she guessed. Circumstances would require that. But some of the British were not so bad. They would have a little house in the country, and she would have her family. Not *Kinder, Kirche, Küche*—her mother's philosophy—because that would be paralyzingly dull. But a family nevertheless. She would work on the farm, riding horses. At night she would tuck in her little girl and read her bedtime stories. Fairy tales; Mother Goose. *Little Miss Muffet sat on a tuffet.*

She brought one hand to her mouth, to stifle a yawn. It was late. She was still hungry. Even the thought of curds and whey was suddenly, obscenely appealing.

Along came a spider, and sat down beside her . . .

A spider, she thought.

She felt a flash of déjà vu. A dream of a memory . . . a memory of a dream. A spider, slipping into her mouth and tickling her tongue. Thirteen legs on that spider.

Her brow wrinkled.

It *had* been a dream, hadn't it? A recent one, not far obscured by the passage of time. And the spider had not been a spider. It had been a hand. A hand with thirteen fingers.

Klinger's hand, pushing something into her throat. *Take your medicine.*

She made a small, confused sound: *Hrm.*

Was there some significance to the dream? It seemed that there must be. A dream, as they said, was never just a dream. And it was almost reachable, almost on the tip of her mental tongue.

Klinger, sitting by her bed, feeding her medicine. But there was something wrong with his hand. She remembered a sense of horror and revulsion. She did not want to swallow the medicine. But swallow it she had; for he had forced her.

The medicine represented something, she thought. In the odd, skewed logic of dreams, it represented something from reality.

The medicine . . .

She caught the distant buzz of an insect. An ear-tricking buzz, both small and large. Gaining volume.

She stood up; the case on her lap spilled to the ground. She didn't notice. Her eyes were searching the sky.

There—coming in under a dark reef of high clouds. The plane.

She felt herself smiling. She had made it. In one more minute, she would be safely aboard. Then back to England.

In one more minute, if nothing went wrong . . .

Then she heard another sound. From the direction of the path that led to town. She turned her head.

A man was climbing the path.

Chapter Seventeen

"Look there," Braun whispered.

Hagen looked. He felt a sudden flare of dismay. Hobbs was coming up the path—and the two agents on that side of the field had let him come too far. The girl had already seen him. He was surrounded by incompetents.

Then he realized that the man was not Hobbs at all; perhaps that was why the agents had let him pass. It was an older man, bent almost double.

"The fisherman," Braun said. "Brandt."

"What's he doing here?" asked the man with the uneven eyes.

"Look," Braun said again, pointing in another direction now.

Hagen turned his eyes. The plane was there, coming in low.

"Herr Obersturmführer. What should we do?"
Hagen hesitated.

Brandt saw the girl and the plane at the same time.

He came to a stop. Nothing to worry about, after all. The extraction was proceeding. His secret was safe.

But there was a feeling: in his blood, in his bones. A premonition. All was not right.

He turned his head, looking for a sign of life in the brush. His eyes were not dependable these days. And the forest was full of mysteries, of insects and birds and trees that concealed things behind their undulating leaves.

Then his eyes moved to the stagnant lake. If there were secrets to be told, perhaps the water would share them with him. The water had been a part of his family's blood for generations upon generations. They were attuned to each other, he and the water, with an intimacy that he would never share with land.

But the lake was still; it told him nothing.

He thought that he saw something on the far bank. A dark shape, or maybe two, among all the other dark shapes near the ground. But he couldn't be certain.

Then his eyes ticked higher. He had seen a glint: in a tree just beyond the edge of the lake. He saw it again, a flash of starlight off metal. A figure with a rifle, aiming it at the field.

Gestapo, he thought.

For one more instant, he stood, torn by doubt. If he cried a warning to the girl, then they would have him, whether or not she managed to get on board the plane. And if they had him, the future would be bleak. The only question would be whether death came quickly or slowly.

But if he held his tongue and the girl didn't manage to get aboard, they might still have him. He was standing in plain sight, clearly visible under the bright night sky.

And if the girl didn't make it back to England, Noyce might let out his secret.

He would prefer death to that overwhelming dishonor.

He raised an arm, drew a breath, and opened his mouth. But he didn't have enough spit to make the word.

He swallowed, moistening his tongue. Then parted his lips again and called at the top of his lungs:

"There!"

The man on the path was pointing.

Eva followed the line of his arm. It led across the field, over the pond, to the trees. *"There!"* he cried.

Then she saw the man in the trees. Holding a rifle.

She gasped, ducking for cover.

Hagen also followed the line of the man's arm. He saw a figure in a tree, brandishing a rifle.

That was Hobbs.

And now the girl had seen him, too. Everything was falling apart, even as he watched, right there in front of his disbelieving eyes.

No. The girl would run for the plane, beset by panic. Even if Hobbs did know the truth, he would never reach her. Hobbs' time was at an end. And Hagen would finish the man himself— making him pay for what he had done to Frick.

He turned to his men, pulling his gun from its holster.

. . .

Hobbs looked down from the sky—the plane was passing right over his head with a long Doppler whine—when the man's hoarse scream echoed out across the lake.

The man, whoever he was, was pointing at him. And now the two agents on the near bank were turning to face him.

Finished, he thought.

But of course he was. He had been finished in the other tree, when the Gestapo agent had been following him. The oddly comforting feeling returned. He had known Death, once upon a time. And now they would become reacquainted. He had known it for his entire life, although he had rarely thought of it. Yet the knowledge had always been there. Someday it would end; and today was as good as any.

No, he thought then. *Not finished yet.*

He raised the Enfield. Five bullets. If he could make them count, he might still reach Eva.

He sent one into the chest of the man by the lake, and the man tumbled backward with a splash.

He worked the bolt. Tracked the second man, who was turning, looking for shelter. He shot the second man in the back.

Worked the bolt.

The plane was coming in for a landing.

Two figures: the man who had pointed at him, who was *still* pointing at him, and Eva. Long-range. He concentrated. Aimed at the pointing man. His hand moved with a sudden nervous spasm. He chewed on his lower lip, fit his finger back over the trigger. Aimed again.

Fired.

The pointing man went down.

Now the plane was moving in to land. No room to spare. *Some daredevil of a pilot*, he thought fleetingly. *Some young fool, willing to give it all for King and Country.*

Two bullets left. And one last chance to get to Eva.

He was preparing to drop from the tree, to make a mad dash across the field, when other men materialized from the foliage behind Eva—three of them.

And he was suddenly aware of two more: rustling on the eastern side of the lake, coming out into view.

And then two others, on the western side, running forward at the sound of the gunshots.

Only two bullets left. So he was finished after all.

But he could do one last thing. He could make certain that Hagen's plan would never come to fruition.

Instead of dropping from the tree, he brought the rifle back to his eye.

And sighted on Eva.

Hagen was moving.

Circling to the west, around behind Hobbs. The man's luck had finally run out, he thought. In a few more moments, Hagen would have him. He would show Hobbs what it meant to interfere with Gerhard Hagen.

Don't make it personal, he thought.

But it *was* personal.

As he moved, he saw the agents flooding onto the field. Not interfering with the girl, but interposing themselves between Hobbs and the plane. Giving her every chance. As long as she didn't realize that was what they were doing . . .

The girl was crouched behind a rock just slightly too small to shield her completely. Hagen had been impressed by the way she had taken cover—it had been born of instinct. She had not panicked. In that instant, he had felt the whisper of a revelation about the woman. He had seen why the British had chosen her as their agent. She was raw, and she was young. But something inside her was made for this. She had talent that could be refined. She would have made a fine pupil.

And now the plane was down, already wheeling around for the takeoff. The girl was breaking from behind her cover, making a try for it.

He saw Hobbs, in the tree, shouldering the rifle again. Not pointing at the SS men on the field, but beyond them, over them.

At the girl.

He couldn't, Hagen thought.

He wouldn't.

But he was.

Hagen moved faster, raising his gun.

William, Hobbs thought. *Are you sure you know what you're doing?*

Spot weld between cheek, hand, and rifle. The night was calm. He had already learned the gun's whimsies. He could make the shot.

Eva was running for the plane. He led her off. His finger tightened on the trigger.

Are you sure you know what you're doing? he thought again.

If he hadn't been sure before, he was now. The SS agents in the field had set themselves between him and Eva. They'd had every chance to apprehend her, and they hadn't even tried. She was meant to get on that plane, as he had guessed.

He fired.

The bullet went high, to the right.

You did that on purpose, he thought.

He chambered the final round.

Now the Nazis were returning fire. Bullets whizzed past him on his left, over his head. His bladder let go, staining the crotch of his trousers; he hardly noticed.

Then Eva had nearly reached the plane. Her arm extended toward a ladder that had been welded to the side. But even as she reached for it, she was looking around, at the SS men scattered across the field. An expression flitted across her face. What was it?

His finger on the trigger paused.

As he watched, the expression deepened, became comprehension. Then he knew: she herself had suspected that something was not right. She had spent enough time with Hobbs to recognize a con when she saw one. And now that the men were letting her go, the pieces had fallen together.

The Lysander was gaining speed. Her expression turned determined. She grabbed again for the ladder, and then she had it.

An instant later she was clambering up the side of the plane. The Lysander was drawing closer, gaining speed. Eva was exposed on the side, pulling herself up, directly in Hobbs' sights. An easy shot.

But his finger relaxed. He lowered the rifle.

There was no need to fire.

Dark relief flooded him. Whether she knew it or not, he had spared her. For him, it was finished—but for her, life was only beginning.

He turned his eyes to follow the plane as it lifted over his head, the engines filling the world.

The plane was heading into the lake.

At the last instant, the pilot pulled back on the throttle. Eva felt the wind being taken from her lungs. She was pressed back into the observer's seat in the rear cockpit, the engines screaming all around her. She could hear herself screaming, adding to the din.

Then the lake was skewing onto its side. They climbed toward the reef of clouds, the land rolling away beneath them.

The pilot turned to look at her. She was surprised at how young the man looked. Her own age, she thought. He was smiling—a complicated smile, of fear and relief and satisfaction.

"I think I pissed myself," he remarked.

She only stared at him.

Two minutes later, they crossed over the coast; the dark sea spread out beneath them, vast and inscrutable.

Hagen approached the tree from behind.

He raised his Luger. Hobbs was facing away, following the plane as it arced above his head. Helpless.

But Hagen couldn't resist. The man had to know who had won. He demanded at least that much satisfaction.

"William," he called.

Hobbs turned his head. The Enfield in his hand began to rise—but the rifle was a large weapon, and a clumsy one; thanks to the constricting branches of the tree, he had no chance of moving quickly enough to save his own life. And he must have realized this. He must have realized that he was finished.

And yet, inexplicably, there was the ghost of a smile on his face.

Hagen shot him three times.

As Hobbs tumbled from the tree, Hagen let out a long, shuddering breath. Then he stepped forward, the Luger held ready.

The Engländer lay on his back, one hand twisted into a grasping claw. But his eyes were glazed; the hand was motionless. The man was already dead.

Yet the ghost of a smile remained.

Hagen emptied the gun into his torso. Then he stepped away, reaching out one hand to support himself against the tree. His headache had returned, pounding viciously.

Too close.

A vacation, he thought.

He would force himself to take a vacation.

He needed one.

Chapter Eighteen

THE WAR OFFICE, WHITEHALL:
APRIL 1940

The five interrogators wore identical charcoal pinstripes.

As each session progressed, their suits became lank with smoke and perspiration; by the end they looked as wrung out as Eva felt. Yet when the next session began, after a few hours of sleep stolen on a thin-mattressed cot or—when Oldfield felt generous—in a small flat they had taken out for her over a bookshop, the suits were crisp again. Were they the same suits, or new ones? Were they pressed and cleaned between each session? Did each man pass his suit to the man sitting on his left? With such questions, Eva distracted herself, and by doing so, she kept her sanity.

One of the men was always writing. She assumed that a microphone was hidden someplace, in this cramped windowless office on the fifth floor of Leconfield House, but the man always wrote anyway. Another of the men was always asking her to repeat whatever she had just said. A third frowned incessantly, as if he suspected Eva was trying to fool them; a fourth presented a façade of patience, understanding, and goodwill. She could trust this one. He was her defense against the others—or so she was meant to feel.

The fifth man was Cecil Oldfield.

Oldfield rarely spoke. Instead, he listened, conveying approval or disapproval with small tacit signals: a plucking at his sideburns, a small dry arching of eyebrows. Somehow, the four men picked up on his signals, and steered the debriefing in whatever direction he was indicating.

When her voice became too hoarse, they gave her sweet tea with lemon and took a five-minute break. Once every six hours, she was allowed to go for a walk around Saint James Park, always in the presence of the watchers. And once every twelve hours, or fourteen, or twenty-four, she was allowed the few pilfered moments of precious sleep.

Now the friendly one, with his open, agreeable face, was asking her for the tenth time to describe Klinger's demeanor on the night he'd appeared on her doorstep and whispered the word to her: *Schlieffen.*

"He was drunk," she started, and the one who always frowned immediately interrupted: "Actually drunk?"

"Yes. I think so."

"Based on what?"

"He smelled of schnapps. And he was slurring."

"But it could have been an act."

"It could have been."

"But was it?"

"I don't think so."

"Go on," he said.

She was allowed to continue until she'd reached the end of her story. Then the one who always asked her to repeat herself asked her to repeat herself.

They wanted to know the contents of the letter Hobbs had passed to her. Each time she tried to remember, she reported the words with slight variations. The frowner—following a cue from Oldfield—seized on this as if it was of great importance. When Eva tried to explain that memory was fallible, that if she reported the same words each time then *that* would have been cause of alarm, she prompted a great amount of throat clearing, doubtful glances, and lighting of cigarettes.

Then they looked at Oldfield, who stroked his sideburns. The frowner said, "We'll get back to that in a moment."

She couldn't tell how they were taking her story. Did they believe her? Or did they think she was part of some Nazi operation? Or did they think she was an honest dupe? Or—

"—how many?" the frowner was asking.

How many SS agents had been on the field, he meant. She shook her head.

"Four? Six? Eight?"

"Six. Or eight."

"More?"

She shrugged. "I don't know, exactly."

"Yet they didn't move to stop you."

"No."

"Perhaps they simply didn't have time. Or perhaps the man in the tree with the rifle kept them still. Were they under cover?"

"At the beginning, they were under cover. Then they came out."

"The man in the tree . . ."

"Hobbs," she said.

"How do you know that?"

"I just know."

"Did you see him?"

"Yes."

"Did you see his face?"

"No."

"Then how do you know?"

Eva shrugged again. "Intuition."

"Intuition," he repeated, with immeasurable sarcasm.

She felt like a slab of butter in a saucepan. It didn't require much warmth to turn butter from a solid to a sizzling liquid; and then, if one lost track and looked away for just a moment, the butter evaporated forever. She wondered if the men recognized that they were running this risk with her—of cooking her for a moment too long, and turning her into something less solid than air.

She mentioned her dream, of Klinger urging her to take her medicine. There was something wrong with the medicine, she said, conscious of the fact that her voice lost force as she tried to communicate this ineffable *something*. There was something wrong with Klinger.

The men sent knowing glances to one another, and seemed just on the verge of snickering.

"Dreams and intuition," her "ally" said as kindly as possible.

"It's just a feeling—"

"Women are emotional by nature," the frowner interrupted. "They're always having *feelings*. But their *feelings* can depend on so many things. Even on the time of the month. Isn't that right?"

She looked at him, amazed. He was looking back pointedly, as if she might actually confirm or deny this. Not, of course, that they would believe her either way.

Then she burst out laughing. Oldfield stroked his sideburns, picked a speck of lint off his lapel, and announced that it was time for tea.

After eight days of debriefing, she was led to a different room.

This was the Director General's office. Oldfield sat behind a vast desk, beneath oil portraits of men who had held his position previously. All of the men wore the same immaculate charcoal pinstripes as Oldfield himself. He made as if to stand when she came into the room—but in reality he rose only to a sort of squat, and waved her into a chair.

He offered tea, looked marginally and inexplicably disappointed when she refused, tented his fingers before his chin, and let a moment fall away.

"I believe you," he said then.

She waited for the qualification, but none was forthcoming. He simply looked at her for a few moments more, then continued: "You've managed to make quite an impact on us. And we pride ourselves, as a rule, on not being swayed by ephemera such as *intuition.* So that's no small accomplishment. There's the matter of the SS men on the field, of course, which helped bring us along—positioned, as the airplane's pilot has confirmed, in such a way that you might have been stopped from reaching the plane. And then there's the ease with which you managed to seduce the OKW clerk in the first place. Not that I mean to imply anything about your capacity to . . ."

He colored a bit, and quickly rushed on.

". . . in any case. It just all falls together rather neatly, doesn't it? A bit too neatly, if you ask me. I'm obliged to report your results to the Prime Minister, no matter what my personal opinion might be concerning their veracity. But I will make it perfectly clear that in my learned opinion, there's something rotten in Denmark."

He smiled at his own small spark of wit; she inclined her head gratefully.

"I apologize for the rough nature of the debriefing," he went on—speaking faster now, as if anxious to get on with the rest of his day. "But we're finished with you now. I'm afraid you won't be able to strike out on your own, however, if that's what you've been expecting. A few naysayers are still of the opinion that you're here at Canaris' bidding. So for the sake of caution, we'll need to keep you under observation."

"Observation," she repeated.

"Never fear. It's a temporary situation. The only alternative is an official inquest, which I assume you'd be just as happy to avoid."

"I . . . yes."

"Once this blows past, there will be several options available to you. A few within this agency, as a matter of fact, if I have anything to say about it. Or you can go about your business as you please. No doubt you'll want to take this opportunity to think carefully about your future, so that when the time comes you'll have a level head. Mm?"

She nodded again.

"I understand that you grew up on a farm in Saxony," he said. "Is that right?"

"Yes?"

"Why not spend a week or two at Plumpton Place, lending a hand with the horses? It will keep the hand-wringers among us at ease. And it might give you a chance to clear your head. Then we might discuss your future with Whitehall."

His expressive eyebrows climbed higher on his forehead.

"If," he said, "you choose to have a future with Whitehall."

By the time May arrived, in an explosion of daffodils and crocuses, Eva had adopted the lazy rhythm of life at Plumpton Place.

She divided her time between an Arabian mare named Necromancer and a collection of Shakespeare that she had discovered in the mansion's dusty library. There was no hand to be lent caring for the horses, despite Oldfield's promise; the stables were tended by an elderly groom who guarded his territory jealously. Eva learned to recognize his ever-present stalker's cap from a distance, and learned to stay away except when she was determined to take Necromancer for a ride.

Yet she felt fairly content with her lot—riding and reading were pleasant diversions—or thought that she did, until one morning when she looked up from her book and noticed, through the window of the drawing room, a young woman strolling across the lawn with a baby in her arms.

The sight jarred Eva more deeply than she would have imagined possible. Her breath caught; suddenly she felt on the verge of tears.

She set the book aside and moved to the window. The woman was completely absorbed with the baby, which was carefully bundled in a blue shawl. This woman, Eva thought, should have been her. In fact this *was* her—in some other world, where life made perfect sense. It was a world where the Nazis had never come to power, where Eva was a struggling but promising young actress who was forever relegated, or so it seemed, to the bottom of the marquee. But there was time for her career to blossom; there was plenty of time. Her husband earned a good enough living. He had given up on just getting by when the baby had been born, at Eva's insistence, and now he worked long but honest hours, doing something with his hands. And she had not lost everything. She was not without a country or a future or a lover. She was this young woman on the front lawn, with many challenges ahead and many loved ones by her side to help her face them.

Then someone stepped into the drawing room behind her. She turned and found herself facing a young man with dark hair and smoky brown eyes, wearing a leather jacket faded almost white. He came toward her with his arms outstretched, as if they knew each other intimately.

When she drew into herself, he faltered. "I'm sorry," he said. "You don't recognize me?"

She shook her head; the implied embrace became a professional handshake.

"Arthur Deacon. I'm the pilot—"

"Oh!" she said. "Forgive me. Of course."

They shook hands. She found herself wishing that she had accepted the embrace instead—but the opportunity, of course, had passed.

"Have you got a moment?" he asked.

As if she had anything else.

He introduced her to his wife and son (the woman eyed her sideways, with the same jealous suspicion manifested by the groom when she came too close to the stables), and then she and Deacon took a stroll around the forest paths.

"I don't suppose you've seen a newspaper," Deacon said. "They keep you to yourself out here, don't they?"

"Yes, I suppose they do."

He walked for another few seconds without speaking. He had his hands jammed into the pockets of his leather jacket, and he kicked at small rocks whenever they presented themselves. "There's something you ought to know," he said at length. "Oldfield would have come himself, but he's got his hands awfully full these days. So he sent me—his favorite nephew. His only nephew, to tell the truth. But therefore his favorite."

Eva smiled. She found herself liking this young man very much. In fact, the affinity she felt bordered on the inappropriate. Did he understand that *she* should have been the one to have his baby? Ridiculous, she thought immediately, and struggled not to blush. It was only because this young man had saved her life that she felt such inappropriate affinity for him. For no other reason than that.

Deacon remained focused on the ground between his feet. "Hitler has made his move," he said. "Five days ago, now."

She knew the rest of it before the words had passed his lips—not the details, but the essence.

"Over a hundred German divisions moved into Belgium and the Netherlands. The French commander, a bloke named Gamelin, rushed the bulk of his armies to repel the attack. He was expecting a drive through the Low Countries and then Sedan. Based, at least in part, on information delivered by the Prime Minister—who chose to ignore the advice of my uncle and his esteemed colleagues."

She nodded, hooking a strand of auburn hair behind one ear.

"Then the Nazis unleashed a blitzkrieg through the Ardennes," Deacon continued. "There weren't many troops left to stop them, and the ones that were aren't worth much. For all practical purposes, it's already over. Chamberlain has resigned—the Labour leaders and the Liberals simply refuse to serve under him any longer. Uncle Cecil may well be tendering his own resignation within the next few days, if he can't find a way to wriggle out of it."

"I tried to tell them," Eva said.

"Yes. Uncle Cecil mentioned something to that effect. A lot of bloody bishes around Downing Street, if you ask me. They've got their heads in the clouds. They simply can't believe that a man like Hitler really exists—one who would lie to their faces, again and again, and smile all the while."

He saw a stone, and kicked it.

"But now," he said, "the real fight begins. Churchill's taken control, and he'll do what needs to be done. We may have lost the battle. But the war is far from over."

For several minutes, they walked in silence. Birds chirruped brightly around them. Then a cloud passed in front of the sun; the day became overcast, the forest a patchwork of grays.

"There's something else," Deacon said abruptly. "You'll let me know, of course, if I overstep my bounds . . ."

She glanced in his direction. "Yes?"

"It's about Hobbs. He was a friend of yours. Wasn't he?"

"A friend," she repeated. "Yes."

"I never met the man myself," Deacon said. "But his reputation was fairly well known. And it was hardly pure. I'm afraid that it doesn't stand much chance of improving in the future, either. In the opinion of those who matter, he's guilty of treason."

She refrained from saying anything.

"But that was him up in that tree, wasn't it? I saw him quite clearly, just as we were taking off."

"It was him"

"Uncle Cecil mentioned that you'd said that as well."

"That's right."

"He looked as if he was aiming that rifle right in your direction. Did you know that?"

She blinked. "No," she said.

"There was a lot going on, of course. I can't be absolutely certain of what I saw. But I had the distinct impression that he planned on shooting you—and then changed his mind."

As they continued strolling, she considered this. It had been at that moment, just as she was climbing onto the plane, that she had first realized for herself the strangeness of the situation. The men spilling out all around, and yet letting her go. And had that showed on her face? It must have.

So perhaps Hobbs had seen this—and he had spared her. For

he had known, somehow, that Klinger had been part of a deception. He had fought his way to the extraction site to warn her, perhaps, that she had been tricked. But then his faith in her—and his love for her—had won out.

She thought there was a ring of truth to that. But perhaps it was just wishful thinking. It was a more pleasant conclusion, after all, than the alternative: that he truly had been using her; that in the end he had been faithful to nobody but himself.

"Who knows?" Deacon asked. "There was a lot going on, as I said. Perhaps my eyes tricked me."

The trail was winding around now, bringing them back in the direction of Plumpton Place.

"In any case," Deacon said, "I personally am of the opinion that he was a decent sort—at the end, if at no other time. I thought you might like to hear that."

"Thank you," she said.

"You may also be interested in hearing this: one of Uncle's oldest friends has expressed some interest in you. He's assembling an operation even as we speak, and he'll be needing a hand—several hands, as a matter of fact. It's to be rather a large undertaking. I was considering signing on myself, since my wife would rather not have me flying."

He kicked at another stone and then looked up at her; his eyes gave a mischievous glint.

"Have you thought about what comes next?" he asked.

HAM COMMON, SURREY: JUNE 1940

Professor Andrew Taylor led Eva into the cell, gestured at the two chairs by the small table, waited until she had sat, and then took the other chair for himself. He was a heavy man, and the wood creaked complainingly when he settled down. He ran a hand through his sparse hair, lit a cigarette, pushed his spectacles higher on his bulbous nose, and began to speak.

"When we arrest the spies," he said, "we bring them here."

Eva began to twist a strand of hair, listening.

"Then we have a go at them," Taylor said. "The goal is to see whether they can be trusted. If we decide that they can, we turn them back out again. They continue spying, under close supervision. We'll use them as the war goes on, you understand. They'll be feeding Canaris exactly what we tell them to feed him. The Nazis may have put one over on us this time—but two can play at that game."

"I see," Eva said.

"We call it Double Cross. The benefits of having a Jerry on the team–and a pretty one, at that—are obvious. When a spy is arrested, he feels many things. Fear. Shame. Perhaps even a measure of relief. In this particular case, I'd like to think that we have right on our side. And I'm hoping that some of the spies we capture will feel the same way. But psychologically, they need an excuse before they turn over. Simply giving in equates to failure. But if we show you as an example . . ."

"An example?"

He took a long drag from his cigarette, gazing at her over the crackling ember.

"You'll play a captured Abwehr spy. You'll be left in a cell

257

adjacent to our new recruits; and during those long lonely nights, you'll strike up a friendship. You'll explain that we've treated you well, since you began to cooperate. Make them feel they can trust us. You might even plant some ideas about Hitler being the worst possible thing for Germany. We'll work on a script for you—and of course, you'll be free to improvise."

His spectacles slipped down; he pushed them up again.

"And for the time being," he said, "that's about it. I know it seems miserable here, but you'll get used to it. Once in a while, if you get too browned off, you might even slip into London for a few hours. Of course, you'll clear it with me first. What do you think?"

Eva caught herself twisting her hair, and made herself stop. After a moment, she reached forward and took one of Taylor's cigarettes. He lit it for her, looking into her eyes.

"It's not quite Royal Victoria Hall, is it?" she said.

"A far cry, my dear. This place was built as a mental asylum, after the Great War. But now it's our home."

"Well," she said. "I suppose one's got to begin somewhere."

"That's a yes, then?"

For some reason, she found herself thinking, all at once, of the girl who had sat reading her book by the harbor at Goth-mund. The girl had reminded her of herself. And she had felt an urge, when she had seen the girl, to go and tear the book from her hands. It was the desire to make something more of herself, after all, that had put Eva into such an unpleasant situation in the first place. It would have been safer to try nothing. Because to try and fail was bad enough; but to try and succeed could be even worse.

Yet that was only one way of looking at it. She could turn the thought around, as if it were a diamond being held to the light.

From a certain angle, the diamond would show only one side: that by striving to make something of herself she had lost everything. But another rotation would reveal another facet, which might mean just the opposite. From this facet, she saw that it was better to try, even if things did not work out just so. Without effort, after all, came passivity; and with passivity came people like Hitler, ready to take advantage.

The peculiar thing was that the diamond could show only one facet at a time. It was perfectly balanced, perfectly symmetrical, and each time one looked at it, one thought one saw the entire truth. But in fact there were many truths, as the diamond was rotated, seemingly at odds with one another, and yet all valid. And it was *right* that one could see only any one truth at a given moment. That was what it meant to be human, in a way. And that was why one required faith—faith that there was more to the diamond than met the eye, and that there was always another side of the stone to be seen.

Taylor was watching her, sitting straight in the chair with the flawless posture of the British. Sometimes it seemed laughable to her, that English propriety. But not at the moment. At the moment, it seemed as *right* as anything ever had. These were not her people; and yet they were, if only she was willing to let them be.

She smiled.

"Why not?" she said.